What people are saying about…

Pulp
Book I – Everlasting Evil

"I can't say that James E. Sarver is the next William Faulkner, but in terms of literary talent, he may well be the next William Shatner."
— *Bob Tillamook, Hopi Indian Reservation Newsletter*

"I didn't want to like this book, and I was not disappointed."
— *Earl Swift, Kiwanis Club Bulletin Board*

"*Pulp Book I - Everlasting Evil* moves along at a frenzied pace from one improbable incident to another. The characters are wooden, the dialogue hackneyed, and the prose stilted like a two-story-tall carnival clown. Still, where else are you going to find so much fun, adventure, intrigue, and excitement? Here's one suggestion: try mowing your lawn."
— *Gina Zumiya, Nation of Islam Press Release*

"It does appear to have been spell-chec&ed."
— *Thomas Bosephus, Small-Time Books*

"The background of this book is a murky mystery, about which the so-called 'Editor & Arranger' refuses to elaborate. Where did he get it? How did he get it? Why did he get it? He won't say. Frankly, I wouldn't be surprised if he made the whole thing up."
— *Harold Fancy, The Dyspeptic Skeptic Magazine*

"I look forward to future volumes with bated breath. Seriously — I refuse to breathe if any more of these are published."
— *Jacqueline Hier, Association of Associated Associates*

Pulp

Book I
Everlasting Evil

From the Papers of
Miles Hudson, Ph.D.

Edited & Arranged
by
James E. Sarver

Pulp
Book I - Everlasting Evil

Copyright © 2007 James E. Sarver

All conceivable rights reserved.

ISBN 978-0-6151-6180-8

Cover Design by Alan Lee

www.pulp-thenovels.com
www.jamesesarver.com

for

pelham grenville wodehouse

EDITOR'S NOTE

The means by which this document came into my possession, I am not at liberty to disclose. Suffice to say the document has a long and troubled history and may well be, in the end, more trouble than it's worth. But the story of Miles Hudson, professor of history, is one that, while it may not precisely *deserve* to be told, at the very least does not deserve to be suppressed. For that reason I have chosen to publish his manuscript, its myriad flaws intact, correcting only minor issues of spelling, punctuation, plot, structure, characterization, theme, and flow. I cannot corroborate its contents; I cannot vouch for its veracity. I am merely a presenter. *Here*, I say unto you. *You* take it.

AUTHOR'S NOTE

Many people were consulted regarding the more technical aspects of this book, too many to list here; but you know who you are (though I did use an alias when contacting certain of you), and I thank you all.

Whatever may be right about this book is a collaborative effort between these persons and myself.

Whatever may be wrong is entirely their fault.

CHAPTERS

CHAPTER I
PROFESSOR OF THE MONTH

DR. FRANKLIN ALLEN HUMPHREYS, DEAN OF CONSTANT COLLEGE, the man who had hired me with no more reference than a lukewarm letter from my Doctoral Advisor, swept a wayward lock of hair from his eye and began everything.

"Good morning, Miles," he said. He was an imposing presence, albeit not physically — his voice creaked with age, and he stooped a little when he walked, and his broad, cherubic face was permanently positioned behind gigantic round spectacles that convinced you he'd break into "Bennie and the Jets" at any moment. But I had seen him, on occasion, by force of personality, by force of his position, command circumstances like a chess master.

An absent-minded, slightly loopy chess master.

"How's everything going?" he asked.

"Good," I answered. "I mean, *well*," I amended myself, remembering my grammar. "Everything's going *well*."

"Any complaints?" asked Dr. Humphreys. "You've been here at Constant nearly seven months now."

I pondered this question as my gaze swept along the shelves of books that lined the walls of Dr. Humphreys' office. His office was, in essence, a used bookstore without the cash register — books on shelves from ceiling to floor, books in tottering piles on the floor, books left open on the desk, books stacked high on two of the three chairs that were meant for visitors. I was no mean reader myself, but Dr. Humphreys lived a life encased in books. A reflection, I mused, on the current state of academe—

But I digressed. I returned to his query. Did I have any complaints? Yes, I thought, I had plenty — no one but me ever replaced the filter in the coffee machine in the lounge, and my students were a disinterested and lethargic lot, and my love life was as empty as my college-mandated Tuesday night "Social History of Women in the 1950's" class — but these concerns, while perturbing, were nothing Dr. Humphreys could do anything about. Except perhaps…the filters?

I said, "Well, the coff—"

"Miles, I wouldn't want you to think that your work here has gone unnoticed. Your reviews have been excellent, from your colleagues to your pupils to the janitorial staff. You're one of the most promising young professors we've ever had the good fortune to hire."

I opened my mouth, but found myself speechless. I didn't think I was a *bad* teacher, but a *great* one? The thought had never occurred to me.

"By way of recognition," continued Dr. Humphreys, who had not even noticed the large O my lips were making, "we have decided to bestow upon you a very special honor."

"…Uhk?" I managed to gurgle.

"Yes. You're familiar, I believe, with the Professor Of The Month Award?"

I nodded dumbly.

"It's highly prestigious, Miles. There is no greater award a professor at Constant College can receive. It may be the highlight of your career."

Great, thought I. *And I'm only 27 years old.*

Dr. Humphreys smiled. "That's right! We have decided that *you* will be the next recipient of the Professor Of The Month Award!"

I tried to smile back at him, but I was too confused to do much other than look at him with a sort of comatose stare — a look I must have learned from seeing it so often on the faces of my students during one of my lectures.

"Well? What do you think, Miles?"

"Er...thank you..."

Dr. Humphreys' expression did not change much, but nonetheless it managed to convey, with conviction, that this was a painfully weak response on my part to what was, after all, news of a terrifically flattering kind.

So I said: "I *am* flattered, Dr. Humphreys. It's just — I'm not sure I deserve it. After only seven months—?"

"Oh, nonsense," said Dr. Humphreys, waving me off. "I can't recall a more deserving honoree."

"Really," I said, hoping it came out more as an exclamation than a question.

"You will be the 1,639th recipient," he said, pride welling in his voice. "Your name will go up there on the wall beside Tunney, and Yarlborough, and Hastings, and — Franklin Allen Humphreys!"

Yes, Dr. Humphreys had won the award himself, at some point in the distant past. I never paid much attention to "the wall," which was located in Steady Hall, in the center of Constant's campus, but Dr. Humphreys' name's enscribement upon that golden, gaudy edifice quickly became known to anyone who spent any time at Constant College.

Recovering a little from my dumbfounditude, I asked, "What is — er — involved in this? A ceremony? Having my picture taken for the *Cry*?"[*]

"It can be as public or as private as you like," said Dr. Humphreys. "We generally hold a small observance on the front lawn of the Administration Building, but that's perfunctory, not obligatory."

(I held my mouth shut tight, for Dr. Humphreys was imparting information that I, had I ever bothered to attend a single presentation of the Professor Of The Month Award, would already have had in my possession. Whether Dr. Humphreys was maintaining a polite silence concerning my lack of attendance at previous presentations of the Professor Of The Month Award, or whether he had not even noticed my lack of attendance, I could not tell. Dr. Humphreys always left the impression that he was both more and less clever than he appeared to be.)

He went on: "If you'd like we can schedule an entire assembly around the award, or I can present it to you here and now with a minimum of fuss. Either way, your name will be up on the wall within the week."

I spoke without hesitation. "I'd prefer a minimum of fuss, to be honest. I'm not very comfortable with public speaking."

"Hmm," he mused. "Odd that you should have chosen teaching as a profession."

A moment passed, then he laughed, to make it clear that he was joking.

Which was good, because I wasn't sure he had been.

---

[*] The Constant *Cry*, the college's bipolar newspaper, which vacillated, often in the same issue, between fawning sycophancy and bitter recrimination regarding the school, the town, the students, the faculty, and the parking situation.

He stood. "So. Miles Hudson. I hereby bestow upon thee the 1,639th Professor Of The Month Award."

He looked down at his desk and rummaged through a pile of books before discovering what he was looking for — a small plaque, the silver faceplate and burnished wood backing of which reminded me of a similar plaque I'd won in the fourth grade spelling bee. Dr. Humphreys held this plaque out to me. "Congratulations."

"Thank you," I said, reaching for it.

As I did so, however, I realized that Dr. Humphreys was not holding the plaque in his left hand, and extending his right for me to shake, but rather the reverse — the plaque was in his right hand, and his left was extended for me to shake.

I eyeballed him curiously. I knew he was right-handed, and anyway, even left-handed people shake hands with their right. Was this another of his eccentricities? Had he, as the editorial page of the *Cry* suggested every other month, finally gone round the bend? Or was this some secret handshake to welcome me into the select company of Those Who Have Been Given The Professor Of The Month Award?

He pushed the plaque forward, urging me to take it. I twisted my right hand inside-out and took hold of his left hand, then shook it hurriedly while simultaneously plucking the plaque from his right hand with my left.

"Thank you so much," I said, modesty incarnate.

But when I glanced up at Dr. Humphreys, what I saw on his face was not the good-natured munificence one would expect from the person from whom one was receiving a noteworthy academic award. What I saw instead was an ill-tempered affrontedness, as if Dr. Humphreys was one of those I'd beat out for the noteworthy academic award.

"Give that back!" he ordered, grabbing at the plaque.

Instinctively I pulled it away. "No!" Then I remembered where I was, and who I was talking to. I handed him the plaque. "Um, here."

He — quite deliberately and methodically — returned the plaque to his right hand, then held out both arms toward me, just as he had before. My eyes darted back and forth between his hands: left, right, left, right, left, right. I was thoroughly bewildered. What did he expect of me? Reciprocity? To shake his left hand with *my* left hand?

It broke all the rules of convention and of civilization. It was an abomination! I could hear my father telling me, as a young boy, "Shake with your right, Miles. *Always shake with your right.*"

But I could also hear my father telling me, "When your employer says 'Jump!', you shouldn't say 'How high?', because you should have already landed."

I pushed out my left hand.

Dr. Humphreys grinned. I'd been correct, I supposed, in my assumption. He was playing some silly game with me, and now that I understood the rules we could conclude without further incident.

I took hold of the plaque with my right hand, took hold of his left hand in my left hand, and pulled the plaque toward me.

Meeting resistance.

Dr. Humphreys stared at me as if I'd just flicked his ear. "What are you doing, Miles?"

Seems I had *not* understood the rules.

"I'm accepting the award," I said.

"Not like that, you're not!"

"I'm not?"

"No!"

Dr. Humphreys sighed, shook his head, and once more re-set the pose that he'd presented twice before: right hand holding plaque, left hand extended to shake.

I was clueless as to how to proceed. What possible arrangement of hands was he looking for? Was I meant to bring a foot into it? What did Dr. Humphreys *want* from me?

I decided to take a risk. I grabbed hold of the plaque with *both* hands, hoping to strip it from his grasp before he could stop me and then exit his office with all due speed. Maybe I'd never get my name up on the wall, but I'd always have the plaque to remind me that my inherent faith in mankind was entirely misplaced.

Dr. Humphreys, however, in spite of his age, was as quick as I was. He, too, held onto the plaque with both hands. We found ourselves in a bizarre pas de deux, arms stretched over his desk, struggling for possession of the plaque, waiting for, any moment, word from King Solomon that the solution was to cut the thing in two.

"Miles, why are you fighting me?" asked Dr. Humphreys, which was not an unreasonable question for him to ask.

"I'm taking my award!" I said.

"If you want this award, you've got to properly accept it!"

"I tried! Twice!"

He peered at me through his glasses. "Miles — I'll give you one last chance. Let go of the award, and receive it from me in the appropriate fashion!"

I yanked on the award, thinking I might catch him off-guard, but he held on tight. I grunted in defeat and released the plaque.

"Fine!" I cried. "Keep the plaque! Keep the award! It's not worth the hassle!"

I stormed out, leaving him thunderstruck behind me. Though I knew I was probably going to be disciplined, possibly even fired, my one regret, as I marched down the hallways of Constant College, was that I never had brought up the coffee filters. These were grown men and women — was it so much to ask that they open the lid of the machine every once in a while?

CHAPTER II
PETER

I WAS NOT HALFWAY TO EVEN HALL, WHERE MY OFFICE WAS LO-
cated, when I heard the resonant call of "Miles, Miles!" following after me. I turned to see a nattily-dressed figure
running toward me, his hand raised high, his bright teeth
flashing beneath a bushy mustaches. Peter Cranston was the
very picture of Mr. Chips.

"Miles, Miles!" he called, breathlessly. He jerked to a
halt and leaned his palms on his knees, drawing in great
gulps of air.

"Yes, Peter?"

He spoke as if he were tapping the message out in Morse
Code. "Why...do...you...walk...so...fast...?...Where's...the
...fire...?"

"I just came from Humphreys' office."

Peter inhaled violently and was, of a sudden, normal.
"Oh, that's right, the Professor Of The Month Award. Congratulations again!"

"Thanks," said I. "Though after what just happened in
there, this may be the first Professor Of The Month Award
given to an *ex*-professor of Constant College."

Peter looked back over his shoulder. "Why, what was
old Humphreys up to this time?"

"I'd be afraid to hazard a guess. I think we may have
been playing patty-cake."

I expected Peter to laugh, or tell me how foolish I was being, but instead he nodded in sympathy. "The poor man can be disconcerting. I remember my first Professor Of The Month Award. I opted for the garden ceremony. This was, oh, sixteen, seventeen years ago. Humphreys started singing bars from 'Turandot,' then stopped in the middle and insisted I finish the phrases for him. It's a good thing I had training in light opera, I can tell you that! —Though it doesn't really train one's lower register, and that's where I've always—"

"What do you mean your *first* Professor Of The Month Award? How many of these have you won?"

"Hm?" said Peter, lost in the glory days of his abandoned theatre career. "Oh, sixteen or seventeen. I've lost count. They only put your name up on the wall once, regardless. I boxed the plaques up — somewhere in the attic, if I remember right. Or the hall closet. My house has so little storage space, for its square footage—"

"Peter, how does a person win the Professor Of The Month Award *sixteen or seventeen times?*"

Peter was nonchalant. "I've been here sixteen or seventeen years."

I gawked at him. I was incredulous. No, I was beyond incredulous. I was beyondulous. I was offended that the award about which I had cared so little had turned out to mean even less than I had cared for it to mean.

If you take my meaning.

Meantime, what I was taking was my frustration, out on Peter.

"How can you have won the award sixteen or seventeen times? What are you, the world's greatest educator?" I shook my head in disbelief. "Your students aren't even all that fond of you! Have you heard what they say about you behind your back? They say, 'Those who can, do; those who can't, teach; and then there's Dr. Cranston.'"

Peter shrugged this off. "In the classroom dislike often equates to respect, Miles. I'd rather be respected than liked."

I started to utter words to the effect of, "Respected my big toe," but thought better of them. Peter was only trying to help, in his clumsy way, and I was upset over something that didn't, in the end, matter that much to me. I was only annoyed on general principle.

"Sorry," I said. "I'm frazzled, is all. I walked out on Humphreys. I didn't even take the award with me."

Peter frowned. "You didn't take the award?"

"No. I...um...I couldn't figure out which hand to use."

"You could at least have taken the award with you. You *did* win it, fair and square."

"I wasn't thinking clearly! Humphreys was acting crazy. Craz*ier*."

"He's harmless, Miles. He's half-senile. And the other half's on medication."

"Well, after what happened, they'll probably take the award back, and I'll be lucky to keep my job."

Peter patted me on the shoulder. "If you could get fired for not playing along with Humphreys, there'd be no one left at Constant. Don't worry, Miles. All will be well. Trust me!"

He'd given me no particular reason to do so, but I do not, by nature, enjoy feeling depressed, and so I grabbed hold of the life preserver he'd thrown me.

"Okay, Peter," I said, with a small smile. "I'll take your word for it."

He slapped me on the back. "There's the Miles we know and love!"

"Why were you charging after me, anyway?"

"Oh, yes!" said Peter. "Almost forgot. It's the — er — the Bonus Prize that you win along with Professor Of The Month."

"Bonus Prize?"

"Yes. In my humble opinion, more valuable than what it supplements."

"No one ever said anything about a Bonus Prize."

"Not every winner gets one, but you do."

"I do? Why me? What is this Bonus Prize?"

Peter's lips curled. "The Bonus Prize is—"

I waited expectantly.

"A date!"

I moved in the general direction of away from him.

"Miles!" he called, chasing after me again. "Miles, this is different! Look, I have a picture of her right here!"

He shoved a two-by-three full-body portrait before my eyes. It pictured a disturbingly beautiful brunette in a tiny, but not tight-fitting, dress, against a backdrop that looked to me to be a cotillion. She was one of the most beautiful women I'd ever seen. She was one of the most beautiful women *anyone* had ever seen. Next to her Helen of Troy was the awkward younger sister.

I gave Peter a squint. "What tragedy befell her after this was taken?"

Peter held up his hands. "Nothing, I swear! She's as pretty now as she was then! If not moreso!"

I should note at this juncture that at the time of this tale I was a single man, in my late twenties, and the only professor, male or female, anywhere near my age at Constant College — and therefore the perennial victim of exactly the type of conduct in which Peter was engaging. The bulk of the faculty, being married, held the opinion that bachelorhood and happiness were two parallel lines that would not, could not, ever meet; thus, their continual attempts to matchmake, generally with some young woman with whom I had nothing in common except an almost supernatural ability to perpetuate an uncomfortable silence.

Peter's attempts at matchmaking had been especially egregious — not one of the dates he'd set me up with had resulted in anything other than poorly-concealed disappointment, and the most recent of them had ended in an ugly scene after an innocent remark on my part that my date's perfume was "unique." She had taken this as a grievous insult and commented that she'd expected to get something more out of the date than conclusive evidence that man did, in fact, descend from the ape.

Peter remained undaunted, however, as witnessed by this latest attempt — while I in turn remained wary, even if the young lady in question was, physically speaking, perfection incarnate.

"Who is she, Peter?"

"My niece."

"Your niece? You have a niece that looks like *this*? Why on earth haven't you tried to set me up with her before?"

"She lives in Atlanta. I never thought of it, until she told me she was visiting, with an eye toward relocating here. She hates the humidity in the south. So do I, to tell the—"

"What's her name?"

"Tara Fury." (Tar-a, as in the La Brea Pits, he pronounced it.)

"How old is she?"

"26."

I flapped the picture in his face. "A woman like this ought not have trouble finding companionship, Peter. What are you hiding?"

"I'm not hiding anything, Miles. Meet her for dinner, find out for yourself."

"You're hiding *something*, I can tell."

"I'm trying to help you! I think you and Tara are well-suited for one another, that's all."

"You thought I was well-suited for that Moroccan woman, and she spent the whole evening denying the Holocaust."

Peter moved on hurriedly, removing a pen from his lapel. "I'll write down Tara's number, you can call her at your convenience."

I glanced again at the picture. "I find it extraordinarily hard to believe that any woman who looks like this" — I held out the photo — "would go for a man who looks like *this*." I framed my own face with my two hands.

Peter looked hurt. "Miles, you underestimate yourself! You're a very handsome man!"

"I'd believe that, if now and then someone other than a 47-year old male professor of English Lit would say it."

"My wife says so, too! *All* the women here think you're attractive!"

"They're all *married*. They'd find Quasimodo attractive, if he took them out to dinner and paid them a little attention."

Peter tugged the photo from my hand as he tucked the scrap of paper with Tara's number on it into my shirt pocket. "Well, you won't hear how handsome you are from Tara if you refuse even to meet her."

I stood silently. The man did have a point. I hadn't been on a date in months. Still, when I had, it had been one arranged by Peter, and I never had gotten the wine stains out of my best shirt.

What I said then is what every person says when they want to say *No* but can't quite bring themselves to.

"We'll see, Peter."
I turned and departed once more.

Chapter III
EVERLASTING HOUSE

I ENTERED MY OFFICE AT 11:04 (I HAD A LARGE CLOCK ON MY WALL) and the call came at 11:09. Dr. Humphreys, said the man on the telephone, wanted to see me.

My immediate thought was that Dr. Humphreys wanted to see me to inform me that he never wanted to see me again. My second thought was that Dr. Humphreys was suffering from remorse about the travesty that had occurred in his office and wanted to apologize in person. My third thought was that Dr. Humphreys would sack me and order me to leave the campus immediately, if not the country. My fourth thought was that Dr. Humphreys, that sweet elderly gentleman, had come to realize how peculiar his actions were, and he was inviting me to a meal, over which he would explain how he'd been debilitated by his increasing dependence on an experimental medicine for rheumatoid arthritis.

And so on and so forth. Anyone looking for the secret to perpetual motion ought to plug a few wires into my brain.

Dr. Humphreys, said the man on the telephone, wanted to see me at his house. Everlasting House, that is — the Dean's Residence — but calling it a "house" was like calling Versailles a "country getaway." Everlasting House was not a house — it was a mansion, a manor, a castle, a palace.

It was built shortly after the college, and by the same man — Patrick Hester, a tycoon of incomparable wealth, taste, and extravagance. The Hester family made its money in timber, and since Patrick in particular was dedicated to higher education (he was a Harvard man), he'd used his wealth to build first the college, in 1919, and then three years later he began work on the house, which was meant to be Patrick's west-coast headquarters. Through the 1920's construction continued, but Patrick never got to enjoy his creation, as he died under mysterious circumstances before it was completed. Rumors at the time were that his sister, Barbara Blanding, had poisoned her brother because of his refusal to indulge her opium addiction.

Whatever the case, Barbara gave the house to her cousin, Roderick Blanding, a staunch and reclusive Methodist who, against Barbara's wishes, went ahead with Patrick's plans for construction. Photos of Roderick showed a kindly-looking man, gray-haired, with intelligent eyes and a pronounced chin. He never married, and never had children, so when he died, in 1953, he left the house to the college, to be used as they saw fit. The Board of Regents debated at length, but in the end Dean Howard Abernathy, a powerful and influential administrator (and allegedly possessor of a large amount of compromising information on his fellow regents) got his way. Everlasting House became the Dean's Residence.

The Dean's Mansion/Manor/Castle/Palace, I mean. Patrick and Roderick had spared no expense in creating the sort of place one normally has to travel to the Black Forest to see, a sprawling expanse of architectural carte blanche next to which one felt not dwarfed, but Lilliputianed. If I were better versed in styles of design, I would describe each of those that met the naked eye from the gate alone, but I do not know my Gothic from my Romanesque, so I shall simply say that if Walt Disney, William Randolph Hearst, and King Arthur had gotten together, their joint creation would not have been anywhere near the caliber of Everlasting House.

I had been here twice before, the first occasion being my first day at Constant College, when the House had hosted a welcoming party larger than a Unitarian wedding, and the second occasion being a fundraising dinner with the Dean and a few select bigwigs from local businesses, churches, and legislative bodies. During these visits I had seen, rounding upwards, one per cent of the House's innards. On this day that percentage was to rise, if not by much, for I found myself being led by Jenkins, the House's Head Butler, through a maze of studies, libraries, conservatories, billiard rooms — around any corner I expected to run into Mrs. Peacock, or Colonel Mustard.

When at last we arrived, I found myself in an oversized room with an arched ceiling and paneled windows and a view like unto that from the space shuttle. Dr. Humphreys sat at a redwood desk that appeared to have been hewn from the General Grant. This was his office, I gathered — if not from the obvious cues, then at least from the nameplate sitting on the front end of the desk, which read "Franklin Allen Humphreys, Ph.D."

Why this nameplate was necessary, here in a private office inside a private home, I couldn't say, and I wasn't about to ask. If I'd learned nothing else during my seven months at Constant — not to mention those ten minutes in his office earlier — I had learned that Dr. Humphreys was a mystery wrapped in a riddle wrapped in an enigma wrapped in a tweed cardigan. He appeared harmless enough, as Peter had indicated, but his reputation was that of a cutthroat administrator who enjoyed a firm stranglehold over his academic power base.

Tread carefully, I told myself. *Don't say anything stupid.*

I won't, I replied defensively. *You just worry about your-self for once.*

Dr. Humphreys rose to greet me as Jenkins bowed ceremoniously.

"Miles," said the Dean.

"Sir," said I.

"Will that be all?" asked Jenkins.

"Yes, Jenkins."

"Very good, sir."

I turned, but Jenkins was already gone. I searched the floor for the outline of the trap door, for there was no other way he could have exited the room so speedily. But I spied nothing.

Dr. Humphreys gestured me to a seat and sat down himself. "Miles, I asked you here for a reason."

"Yes, sir?"

"I would like to apologize to you. My comportment this morning was abominable. Reprehensible. Inexcusable. Don't you agree?"

"..."

"I want to make it up to you." He reached into a desk drawer and lifted a ring of keys. "Here," he said, extending the keys to me — in, of all things, his right hand.

"What are those, sir?"

"They're keys, Miles."

"I know, sir, but — what to?"

"The house. —Well, this one's for the house. This one's for the carpark, and this one's for the front gate, and this—"

"Dr. Humphreys," I interrupted, "are you going on vacation? If you need a caretaker—"

"No, no," said the Dean, waving his arm, jingling the keys. "I'm not going on holiday. I'm *giving* you the house, Miles."

"…"

"I feel simply awful the way I treated you. Please — accept my heartfelt apologies."

He proffered the keys once more.

"Sir, I — I can't accept your house. I accept your apology, but — I can't accept the house, for heaven's sake!"

"You don't want the house?"

"I would love the house — who *wouldn't* love the house? — but I can't just let you *give* it to me."

Dr. Humphreys eyed me up and down. "Too good for it, are you?"

I was aghast. "No, sir! Not at all! If anything, this house is too good for me! This house is too good for Mother Teresa! —But not too good for *you*, of course—"

He changed his tone. "I am including *all* of it. The lake, the golf course, the polo grounds, the mews—"

"Sir, really. I must decline."

He looked down. "You may as well accept, Miles. I've amended my will, here this morning, making you my sole beneficiary. I've contracted a degenerative bone disease. I'll be dead within the year."

My voice was chiding. "You're in perfect health, sir."

"Are you calling me a liar? Me, whose bones could snap, if a breeze came up?"

"Dr. Humphreys, you don't even own the house. The college does. You couldn't bequeath it to me if you wanted to."

His eyebrows came together. Evidently he hadn't thought this through all that well. He stammered for a moment, then his eyes lit up with an idea. "Oh! The upkeep! The upkeep is atrocious! It's driving the school bankrupt. —Yes, this house has bankrupted Constant College!" He sniffed and wiped away a pretend tear. "It's a tragedy, it truly is. But perhaps, out of our tragedy, you can forge a new future."

I had become somewhat impatient. "Might I make a suggestion, sir? Sell one of the Rembrandts in the basement, you'll have more than enough to keep the house going for another hundred years or so."

His gaze was that of Napoleon, or Hitler, after hearing the word *winter* — frustration to the degree of n. His tone changed again, to a flustered pragmatism. "You won't take the house no matter what I say, will you, Hudson?"

This was the first time since we'd known each other that the Dean had used my last name. I'd always been just plain old Miles. We'd come a long way, in a short conversation.

I answered, "No, sir. No, I won't take your house. I sincerely wish I could, but I can't." I asked this next question the way a child asks his father where babies come from. "Dr. Humphreys — why are you offering me Everlasting House?"

He pointed a bony finger at me. "It'll make quite a bedtime story for your grandchildren, Hudson! How you came *this* close to Everlasting House! How they came *this* close to growing up in the lap of luxury! How their lives could have been so much different! So much happier! But *no!*"

"Sir—"

"I've heard enough! Now *go!* Jenkins!"

I felt the butler's presence behind me as soon as his name had finished bellowing forth from Dr. Humphreys' lips. I twisted around and inspected him: impeccable and inscrutable. There was no sweat on his upper lip from sprinting through hallways, no dust on his shoulder from navigating secret underground passages, no rip in his coat from where the trap door caught him as he crawled out. Could the man teleport?

"Yes, sir?" he asked Dr. Humphreys.

His employer's voice was cold. "Escort Hudson here to the front gate."

"That's really not necessary, sir," I said. "It's not necessary," I repeated to Jenkins.

Jenkins did not look at me. Jenkins looked only at Dr. Humphreys.

"You know your way?" asked the Dean of me.

"Yes, sir. Left, three doors, right, down the stairs, right, across the bridge, through the aviary—"

"We won't be needing you after all, Jenkins. You may go."

Anticipating the finale of Dr. Humphreys' sentence after hearing its beginning, I never took my eyes from the butler, determined to discover his secret. But Jenkins merely walked to the door, straight-backed and elegant, and exited.

My brow — not for the last time during this entire affair — furrowed in confusion.

"You may go, too, Hudson."

"Yes, sir," I said. I walked to the door — not as elegantly as Jenkins, I'm afraid, and my back was curved like a bowstring with the weight of the weirdness of the day — and exited.

In the hallway outside, I paused to collect my frayed-to-a-tatter nerves. My calm and ordered existence was fast becoming an anarchic, bewildering mess. Was this what it was like to experience a nervous breakdown? Not on *my* part, mind you, but on Dr. Humphreys'? What on earth else *could* explain his (to understate the case) aberrant behavior? Senility? Insanity? Drugs? Alcohol? A sharp blow to the head?

I had a sudden brainstorm. I glanced around. Of Jenkins — or of anyone else — there was no sign. I was alone outside the door to Dr. Humphreys' office. Being so, I was inspired to put to use a lesson I had learned from too many childhood hours watching police/detective/adventure shows on television.

I put my ear to the door and listened.

CHAPTER IV
WHAT I HEARD

I HEARD THE CRINKLE OF LEATHER, AND THEN A SOFT RHYTHMIC whirring, a sound I didn't immediately recognize, despite the fact that it was in hopes of hearing this exact sound that I had put my ear to the door. I hadn't heard a rotary phone being dialed in years; but I had noticed one on Dr. Humphreys' desk.

His voice said, "This is Humphreys."

Axiom: A subordinate *shall* make a telephone call to his/her superior after he/she receives a visit from the hero/heroine of the police/detective/adventure show.

This confirmed three suspicions of mine: one, something strange was going on; two, Dr. Humphreys was a subordinate, a taker of orders, not a giver of orders; and three, I was cast in the role of hero.

The cumulative depressatory effect of these three facts was almost enough to make me run screaming into the indoor gardens.

But I composed myself and instead listened closely.

"The fish," said the Dean, *"did not take the bait."*

Long pause.

"Isn't this Area Code 555, 555-5555?"*

---

* This is not, it goes without saying, the actual number. Another trick picked up from TV.

Another pause.

"My goodness, they must have given me the wrong number."

Loud ringing-off.

Loud re-dialing.

"Hello? This is Humphreys. *The fish did not take the bait.* I repeat, *The fish did not take the bait.*   ...This *is* the reserve number, is it not? You know who I am? Good. *The fish did not take the bait.* It's a code phrase, I would think. I don't know what it means, either. It's what I was told to say if Miles would not take the House. —Oh, well, then, that's what it means. The House is the bait and Miles is the fish. *The fish did not take the bait.* Yes, makes perfect sense, when you think about it. —I beg your pardon. I am the Dean of a large college, sir. I don't spend my days pondering the subtle meanings of obscure code phrases. Please forgive me, I beg you! —Look, what's your name? I don't find that funny. That is not funny in the slightest. Stop laughing. If you do not stop I *will* hang up. And I *will* tell your superiors. You can't man the phone twenty-four hours a day, eventually I'll get hold of someone else. —You don't value your position much, do you? —My voice may not be frightening, but my influence will be, you little — *he hung up!* He hung up on me!"

Very loud ringing-off.

Very loud shuffling through desk drawers.

"Ah-hah!"

Very loud re-dialing.

"Hello? Oh, good day to you, too. Eh? Oh, I'm fine, thank you. How are you? That's nice. Is this the emergency number? Thank God. This is Dr. Humphreys. *The fish did not take the* — yes, from Constant College.   Why, thank you.

That's kind of you to say. Yes, I do have a message: *The fish did not take the bait.* You'll pass it along? Thank you! Well, you know, they gave me the wrong number, and then I phoned the reserve number, and I've never been treated so rudely in all my life! He said his name was Alexander Graham Bell, but I wouldn't be surprised if it wasn't. Yes, throaty, and gravely, and phlegmy, like George C. Scott. Not like yours at all. Yours has a remarkably pleasant quality. Like a tinkling stream in the Swiss Alps. Oh, I could listen to you all day! Might I ask your name? —Certainly I would! When is good for you? Next Tuesday? Well, where are you located? Oh, of course, I understand. But you know where I'm located, don't you? Any problem getting here? Fine, I'll see you then. Yes, I'm looking forward to it, too. Thank you. All right. You have a good day now!"

Very quiet ringing-off.

"My goodness. One second life seems cold and bleak and empty and the next it's brilliant and warm and delightful! I feel so — *alive!* I feel so — *good!*

A click, as of an intercom.

"Jenkins! Bring my field glasses! I'm going *bird watching!*"

CHAPTER V
THE UNKNOWN

MY NEXT CLASS WAS AT TWO O'CLOCK. I ARRIVED WITH THREE minutes to spare, primarily because I had not been completely honest with Dr. Humphreys about remembering the way out of Everlasting House, and my mind, aswirl, ajumble, akimbo, was hardly in a condition conducive to extricating itself from the modern-day equivalent of the maze at Knossos. Gingerly opening doors, cautiously lifting windows, quietly tapping walls for hollow spaces, steadily cramping my foot muscles during an hour and a half of tiptoeing, my mind had ample opportunity to dwell on the day's macabrities.

I could add three more items to my List of Suspicions Confirmed:

One, Dr. Humphreys belonged to an organization — an organization so organized that it employed code phrases and provided not one, not two, but *three* telephone numbers for its underlings to make their reports. The Mafia? No. Central Intelligence? No — Dr. Humphreys, like most academics, thought less of the CIA than he did of the SS. Unless that was a clever cover...let's see, who else? FBI? MI6? KGB? The possibilities were endless, though I felt safe in confining them to three-letter acronyms.

Two, this organization had a heartfelt desire for me to take up residence in Everlasting House. *Why*, for heaven's sake? What oblique, arcane, cryptic excuse could there be for this organization's wanting me to take Dr. Humphreys' place as head of the Household? It was crazy, it was inexplicable, it was absurd.

Three — and of this I was now positive — Dr. Humphreys was off his nut.

*   *   *

My two o'clock was a course entitled "Civilization Since The Renaissance." It wasn't my favorite three-hour block of the week, but in teaching, you soon learned to rationalize that any given class could have been a lot worse than it was. For whatever reason, the students this semester were, to say the least, more zealous than most — every last one of them possessed a perfect attendance record, and during class discussions every last one of them displayed all the reserve of a trader on the floor of the New York Stock Exchange.

Our topic that afternoon was the Dutch Revolution, a subject that does not excite pupils to the degree that the French or Russian Revolutions do, but does not bore them to the degree that German Intellectual History or Feudalism do, either. So I was startled when, after each of my discussion questions, the horizon of the classroom's landscape was unmarred by students' arms arisen, virtually vibrating with impatience to share some such or other preternaturally salient point. In this class, the landscape was *always* marred, even when I hadn't asked a discussion question.

Finally I blurted, "No one has anything to add?"

Mrs. Jeanne Cosgrove, a woman of magnificent girth and the reddest cheeks this side of Mrs. Claus, meekly elevated her right hand. You must understand that for Jeanne Cosgrove to do anything *meekly* was akin to the sun not rising. It simply didn't happen, and if it did, it was a sure harbinger of catastrophe.

"Yes, Jeanne?"

She glanced around at her fellows, and bit her lower lip, and, her face screwed up as if expecting divine retribution, said, "Uh, Dr. Hudson." She glanced around again, but the looks on her fellows' faces said, *Madam, you are on your own.* "Today's the, er, today's the day for our, er, our papers."

She referred to their term papers, the topics of which were due that day. I had not forgotten; I was putting it off until five minutes or less of class time was left, thereby to avoid precisely what followed.

"Don't we need to tell each other what our topics are?" asked Jeanne Cosgrove. "What if two of us are doing the same thing?"

She was correct, of course. It never ceases to amaze me, that humanity has endured over three thousand years of recorded history only to have created, in toto, seven topics for college history term papers. The seven aren't always the same — in recent years Martin Luther King, Jr. has taken over the slot previously held by Gandhi — but there are always only seven.

The odds of two or more persons choosing the same topic in a class of sixteen, therefore, are 1:2.85714, and the only way to win with that horse is to bet against it — which is what I'd been doing ever since my first experience having students announce their topics in class, when two fistfights had broken out. My policy now was to collect topics in secret, examine them, and calmly and coolly ask those of the identical choices would they kindly choose another that was *not* on The List Of Seven. Disappointment and grousing inevitably resulted, but a college student who isn't disappointed and grousing is either drunk or wearing a cap and gown.

This policy had been, until now, failsafe.

But now...now it was too late. Jeanne Cosgrove had spoken.

She spake once more:

"I'm preparing a study of English politics," she said, which was strange, as English politics was not only not one of the seven topics, but was not on the reserve or emergency lists, either. "I am going to prove that Margaret Thatcher's election was the direct result of Henry VIII's anti-popery."

I believe my lower jaw was somewhere around my waist, but the class was nodding enthusiastically, patting Jeanne on the back, commenting to one another congenially, "I wish I'd thought of that."

"Wait wait wait!" said Mr. Tomkinson, a short, skinny, bespectacled sort. Jeanne Cosgrove, it seemed, had given the boulder a push, and now it was rolling down the hill faster and faster, collecting layer upon layer of fresh snow.

"I have chosen to investigate the origins of a rather famous and popular book," said Mr. Tomkinson, once again demonstrating his irritating habit of preceding his proper nouns with sensational descriptive phraseology. He swept his eyes across the room, lording his special knowledge over us. *The Bible,*" he revealed at last in a near-whisper. "I have done a tremendous amount of research into this, and I am prepared to state unequivocally that the best-known book of all times, the Christian Bible!, was in point of fact written by — *the Japanese.*"

My lower jaw was pendulous before my knees. The class, at least, was not nodding enthusiastically this time — but they were quietly reverent, as if in the presence of Thucydides.

"Not only that," said Mr. Tomkinson, wagging his finger, "but they still own the rights!"

Now the class nodded — but for Jeanne Cosgrove, whose icy expression denoted her discontent at being so rapidly upstaged.

"My topic," put in Mr. Martinez — the boulder was rolling, tumbling, thundering, unstoppable — "is Viking science. Did they or did they not discover electricity?"

This continued for a time, twelve more topics, on the order of Beethoven's eardrums were removed in his sleep by a jealous Mozart, or Lincoln lived and killed Seward in a duel in 1867 and stole his identity and it was he who engineered the purchase of Alaska for seven million dollars. The snowball grew, and grew, the size of a small moon, until it smashed against a mountainside and exploded into a thousand tiny pieces — a mountainside by the name of Bruce Washington.

Bruce was a quiet man, long-haired, with eyes that jumped to and fro like a bird's head, and a T-shirt that was stretched to its limit over what was not so much a beerbelly as a distillerybelly. Bruce was last to share his topic (need I note that for the first time in one of my classes no two students' were the same?) and when his turn came he took over the room like Sinatra in his heyday. His eyes glared at each of us, individually and corporately (at the same time, it seemed), his stare the intensity of a laser beam. He spoke in a voice dogs would have had trouble hearing. "My paper's on THE UNKNOWN, man."

"The Unknown?" asked Jeanne Cosgrove.

"No, man, THE UNKNOWN."

That's how he said it, so that a person could *feel* the capital letters; and yet they were small caps, as if THE UNKNOWN was conflicted about advertising itself.

"THE UNKNOWN?" I said, trying to enunciate appropriately.

"Yeah, man," Bruce said. "You got it."

I did not *get* anything, but that is not something a professor should say to a student. Instead I repeated, "THE UNKNOWN?"

"It's all *over*, man. It's *everywhere*."

Manifestly Bruce had been unsuccessful in convincing anyone in his life that THE UNKNOWN truly existed (why, I couldn't imagine) and now that the class had made the appalling mistake of showing an interest, he was going to play it for all it was worth.

"What is it?" asked Jeanne Cosgrove.

Bruce broke into a routine that he'd most likely rehearsed and delivered into a mirror dozens, if not hundreds, of times. "It's been goin' on for who knows how long, man. Secret...hidden...behind the scenes...you know what they're after? The *world's* what they're after, man! World domination! Total control! Unlimited power!"

"THE UNKNOWN is a conspiracy?" queried Mr. Tomkinson.

I rolled my eyes.

Bruce did not miss a beat. "Doctors. Lawyers. Indian chiefs. Rich men, poor men, beggarmen, thiefs. Some of 'em don't even know they're involved. Take a look around. Your friends. Your neighbors. You never know, man. You *never, ever* know."

"Well," I said, and this was actually true, "we can hardly wait to see your paper, Bruce."

He stared at me. He was frightening, but in a non-threatening way. He whispered, "You don't believe me, do you, man?"

I took a deep breath. "I'm a rationalist," I said, injecting several thousand more ccs of logic into this conversation than it deserved. "If you can prove there's a worldwide conspiracy of doctors, laywers, and Indian chiefs, then I'll believe it. If you can't prove it, then I won't believe it."

Bruce chuffed a snort. "Man, this thing is *big!* If the JFK thing is a grain of sand, this thing is the whole rest of the universe! What do you mean, *proof*? What do you think, they type up their plans and leave 'em out for anybody to find? *Proof!* You don't know much about THE UNKNOWN, man!"

I thanked God and dismissed the class.

CHAPTER VI
HERALDS

MY APARTMENT LAY A FEW MILES FROM THE SCHOOL, IN A TWO-STORY building situated in a copse of pine trees that thoroughly obstructed, all year round, what should have been a spectacular panorama of the valley that held the school and, beyond, Everlasting House. I lived on the second floor, the three or four up-and-down-the-stairs daily supplying me with a small amount of regular exercise that kept me from putting on too much weight regardless of how often I skipped visits to the gym — which also supplied me with a perfect excuse to skip visits to the gym.

The apartment, a studio, consisted of one large room, the living room/library/TV room/office, and two small outcroppings that housed the kitchen and the bathroom. I slept on a futon that had been a gift from my mother and father, who preferred it to take some work, if you know what I mean, for me to get into bed — though, as indicated, they needn't have worried, since my love life after leaving their house had remained in much the same state as it had been while I was in their house. (Viz., non-existent.) Other than the futon, I didn't have much furniture: a computer desk, a small TV, an over-populated bookshelf. The place wasn't compulsively neat, but it wasn't a total mess, either. I would have wanted to clean up a little if a date was coming over, or maybe my parents, but if it were friends? Eh. It's no great effort to move a newspaper out of the way before you sit down.

I came in, tossed my briefcase on the futon, and checked my answering machine for messages. The red light blinked twice, stop; twice, stop. The first message was from an ex-student who regularly called to debate controversial points of history. I made a note to call him back sometime when I had exhausted every other conceivable course of action open to a living human being. The second message was a voice, obviously disguised, but nonetheless a plain, uninteresting voice. It said:

"Hudson. You're in danger. I'm a friend. Let's meet. Tonight. Eight. Papagozzi's."

I was grateful, when the voice had finished, that it was such a dull voice, for otherwise I might have collapsed into a shriveled, cowering ball. The Professor Of The Month Award...left hand, right hand, right hand, left hand...Everlasting House...Jenkins...*The fish did not take the bait*...THE UNKNOWN...*You're in danger*...I had no reason to believe that each of these things was connected, yet at that moment they all coalesced into a single malevolent mass.

My chest thumping, I checked the kitchen and the bathroom, pushing open the door to the latter as would a policeman who's heard a shot from inside. It's not easy to feel threatened when you're alone in a studio devoid of hiding places, but my brain accomplished the task without even, metaphorically speaking, putting its back into it.

When I was satisfied that the apartment was free of Thuggees, ninja assassins, and Russian mobsters, I reached for the phone and dialed.

"Hello," came the answer after four rings.

"Hello," I said.

"Miles? How are you, old boy? Get your award today?"

Hearing this particular voice — the voice of my best friend in the world — had always done wonders for my mood, my attitude, my outlook; but on this day it did nothing for me. I was sinking fast into a morass of fear.

"You there, old man?"

"I'm here."

"What's up?"

"Nothing," I lied. "I feel fine."

Even I could hear the tremble in my throat. I sounded like a turkey on a bumpy road.

"Glad to hear it, old bean!"

Leave it to my best friend in the world to sidestep a clue Inspector Clouseau couldn't have missed. Flynn did not have, or need, a job, since he'd invented some doodad in his early teens that had brought him untold wealth. When we met in college, he'd already perfected his happy-go-lucky devil-may-care man-about-town image; I never got a look at his transcripts, but seeing as, to my knowledge, he didn't attend a single class during four years of school, he must have thrown around a considerable amount of that wealth in order to secure that Liberal Arts degree. He had followed me around after college, bouncing from one interest, one passion, to another, with all the regularity of the tide — indulging his zeal until it was spent, which was usually about a fortnight, and then moving on to the next item on his list. Flynn was a jack-of-no-trades, master of all.

"Why don't we do something to celebrate?" he suggested. "A round of golf, perchance?"

Flynn's passion this fortnight was golf.

"Flynn," I said, "even professional golfers do not celebrate success by playing a round of golf. They go out, they have dinner, they see a show—"

"You want to see a show?"

"It's just an example."

"Dinner, then?"

"That was another example."

"But you *don't* want to play a round of golf."

"I can't, Flynn. I have a…meeting tonight."

(I am not an accomplished liar. By which I mean, I am accomplished at lying, but I am not accomplished at getting away with it.)

"What time is your meeting?" asked Flynn.

"…Eight."

"Oh, my, old thing! Plenty of time to squeeze in eighteen!"

"I don't think so, Flynn."

"You couldn't…postpone…this meeting?"

"Er — no, sorry."

"It's not a date, is it? You don't have a date, do you?"

I sighed. Flynn knew of my history with women. In fact a significant portion of my lack of success in that department could be laid at his doorstep. The few girlfriends I'd managed to keep for any length of time, Flynn had critiqued with abandon, invariably discovering innumerable insuperable flaws. When it came to rooting out infidelity, alcoholism, drug addiction, or communist tendencies, Flynn was without peer. He was my romantic guardian angel.

I lied again, "It is not a date. It is a meeting."

"Well, what are you up to tomorrow? All-Day Passes can be quite affordable—"

"I'm working tomorrow, Flynn. Unlike some, I am employed."

"What about old Humphreys? Did you remember to ask?"

A thought struck me, and that thought was, Oops.

"No, I — forgot. I'll ask him when I see him again."

"They say the greens are like putting on ice!" said Flynn. A noise emanated from the telephone that I assumed (and hoped) was Flynn licking his lips. "You simply *must* request a round, Miles — they won't deny it to a Professor Of The Month winner!"

Flynn's greatest desire, at least during the past couple of weeks, had been to play the course at Everlasting House. He had greeted the text message I'd sent him earlier in the day about my winning the POTM Award with the same ardor with which Gawain greeted a Grail sighting, thanks to the Award's inherent possibilities toward influencing Dr. Humphreys into allowing me and a guest (e.g., Flynn) to accompany him on a round of eighteen at the House.

Thinking about the House led me around again to Dr. Humphreys' unfathomable behavior, and Bruce Washington's paranoiac ravings, and the enigmatic telephone call...the telephone...I was on the phone with Flynn, wasn't I? In the midst of my meandering daydreaming, I'd forgotten what I was doing, but it hadn't helped that total silence had spread across the phone line — I could no longer hear Flynn. Had *they* gotten to him? Even now, did *they* have their mitts on my best friend? Just who were *they*, anyway? I was falling into a near-panic, imagining all sorts of scenarios wherein "the organization" had taken my best friend in all the world and was submitting him to the most heinous forms of torture — but toward what end? *Toward what end?*

Then Flynn's voice returned, and I went back to my usual meandering daydreaming, which generally involved my reclining in a hammock somewhere in the South Pacific. Most men lead lives of quiet desperation; I led a life of a desperate search for peace and quiet.

Flynn asked: "What was your reason for calling, old hat?"

"To talk," I said too quickly. "Catch up on the day."

Flynn paused, then spoke reprovingly. "Always best to share your troubles, old yip. Four shoulders can carry what two shoulders can't."

I wasn't sure whether Flynn had finally caught on that I was one loud noise away from institutionalization or whether he was stating a generic aphorism that had no specific application to our distinctive set of circumstances. I will say, though, that regarding this particular aphorism, Flynn did practice what he preached — not one problem surfaced in his life that I had not heard about within the hour. But I will further say that it was easy for Flynn to practice what he preached, as the most difficult problem that had yet surfaced in his life was a recurring tendency to slice out of fairway bunkers.

"I'm fine, Flynn, really."

"Very well, then. Talk to Humphreys soon!"

"I will."

"Good night, old chum."

"Good night, Flynn."

I hung up. Flynn was my best friend in the world, but he could be as oblivious as a blind man at a silent movie. He'd offered no solace in my hour of need, and, worse, he had reminded me of the promise I'd made him a few days earlier — that I would ask Dr. Humphreys about a round of golf at Everlasting House's famous course. I hadn't thought I would have to keep the promise; I had taken it for granted that Flynn's infatuations would wane, as they always did, and then glom onto another target. But so far his golfical fervor had remained stubbornly stable, and did not look to be cracking for a while yet...which left me with the unpleasant, unthinkable prospect of facing Dr. Humphreys again.

I sank me even further into the Morass of Fear.

I glanced around my apartment again. I had, eons ago, planned to spend the evening alone, listening to quiet music, making ready the spring finals for my classes, reading over the first drafts of Ancient History papers, preparing lecture notes for the next week. In other words, a typical evening for me, an evening like hundreds of others during the year.

Rummaging through my briefcase, I came upon a fresh notebook I'd taken from the college's office supply closet the previous day. I pulled out one of the eighteen different pens inhabiting the case and sat down on the edge of the futon. The words spilled onto the lined page:

Professor Of The Month Award
Everlasting House
The fish did not take the bait.
You're in danger.
THE UNKNOWN?

The words stared back at me like yellow-eyed predators in a moonlit jungle. I was too rattled to discern even the most obvious of connections between them, much less the over-arching pattern behind them.

I should have guessed then that these, the peculiar occurrences of the day, were no mere random happenstances. I should have guessed then that these peculiar occurrences were heralds of a major turning point — that my life had reached a crossroads. That, for a long while at least, there would be no more quiet nights of schoolwork and soft music.

But, to paraphrase Mick Jagger, I could not foresee these things happening to me.

I set down the notebook and pen. I stood and stepped toward the kitchen—

The doorbell buzzed, its sudden sound screeching through the stillness of the night.

I screamed like a little girl and clutched my heart.

Oh, for heaven's sake, I told myself, *stop being so jumpy. It's just the doorbell! Thuggees, ninja assassins, and Russian mobsters don't announce themselves by ringing the doorbell. They announce themselves with the point of a knife, or the barrel of a gun, and by the time you realize they're there, you're already dead.*

You know, I replied, *you're not helping much.*

But if it wasn't Thuggees, ninja assassins, or Russian mobsters, who could it be, at this late hour? All of the non-criminal element was safe at home in bed, or watching TV, or listening to soft music while grading papers.

I grabbed a stapler from my computer desk and crept toward to the door.

What are you going to do? I asked myself. *Staple them to death?*

Shut up, I answered. *A staple in the right place could kill a man.*

You, maybe, said myself.

I peered through the peephole. Framed there in the fish-eye lens, literally larger than life, was the second-most beautiful woman I'd ever seen. Dark hair, dark eyes, sun-browned skin, and a tiny but not tight-fitting dress—

Hold on. The second most beautiful woman I've ever seen is the first *most beautiful woman I've ever seen.*

At my door was Peter's niece, Tara Fury.

CHAPTER VII
TARA

SHE LOOKED JUST LIKE HER PICTURE. UNCANNILY SO. SHE TRANS-fixed my sight — I couldn't look away. Her straight black hair flowed back across her shoulders, down over — could that be the same dress as in the photo? Her brown eyes stared into mine as deeply, it seemed, as mine were staring into hers. The line of her face curved out along her forehead, in along the bridge of her nose, out again in a pert little upturn. Her cheekbones…well, I could go on and on, but take my word for it, the woman was a vision.

…But the vision began to flicker, and fade. Wavy lines snaked around her as if she were standing on the other side of the tarmac.

She flashed out of existence, and then flashed back into existence. What my eyes beheld afterward, however, was not the same Tara with the dark hair and the tight dress.

No, this Tara Fury was shorter, and blonder, and wore glasses, and Levi's.

It was then that I realized that Peter's photograph of his niece had borne an unnatural resemblance to Vivien Leigh.

Unnatural, as in exact.

My brain, overexcited and underdeveloped as it was, had filled in the blanks of Tara's appearance, based on her photo — the peephole in the apartment door had always been murky as a lagoon bed, and I couldn't have seen anything more through it than the vague outline of what may or may not have been an upright human being.

I opened the door and stood there for a moment stupidly.

This new Tara was not ugly by any means, but she was no Vivien Leigh.

"Ready to go?" she asked. For someone from Atlanta, her voice was surprisingly free of an accent; this tidbit did reach my disconcerted mind. If anything, she sounded more northern than I did.

"Sorry?" I mumbled.

"Are you ready to go?"

"Ready to go?"

"Yes."

"Ready to go where?"

"Uncle Peter suggested Briley's, or Papagozzi's. Papagozzi's is supposed to have the longest salad bar in the state, he said. And I could go for Italian."

"It's not Italian," I said by rote, "it's Chinese. "I don't know why they call it Papagozzi's, it only confuses everyone. But they do have the longest salad bar in the state."

"A salad bar? In a Chinese restaurant?"

"That confuses everyone, too."

She laughed. "I guess you all live in a state of Constant confusion!"

I tried not to laugh with her, but I couldn't help myself, because it was kind of clever, so what came out was a conspicuously unmanly titter. Quickly I pretended it was the start of a cough and was soon expectorating like an emphysemac in a boiler room.

"You okay?" asked Tara.

"Y-yes," I hacked, feigning a gradual recovery. "Your — your picture — Peter showed me a picture — a photograph — it — it wasn't — you—"

She giggled. "Uncle Pete's a joker. Don't you know that, working with him so long?"

No, I did not know that. Peter wasn't a joker, he was an evil man with a tragically handicapped grasp of what attracted one unmarried person to another. But I kept silent on the point. Why trample the poor girl's misconceptions about her sadistic Torquemadan uncle?

Tara batted puppy-dog eyelashes. "Disappointed?" she asked.

Mentally, I nodded. It wasn't her appearance that disappointed me, for this new Tara was quite cute, and it wasn't as if Vivien Leigh would ever have given me a second glance. No, what disappointed me was the, for lack of a better word, *vibe* that I received from this new Tara Fury — for, in 27 years of singleness, I had learned to read a woman almost immediately. By which I mean, I had learned to judge, within moments, whether a given female and I had even the remotest chance of eternal happiness together.

You may say, "Miles, you cannot possibly make a truly considered judgment regarding a lifetime of wedded bliss based on two minutes of personal interaction."

To which I retort, "Watch me."

I could not, however, come right out and say this — having convictions is one thing, having their courage is another. So I smiled the toothy grin of the inbred and said to Tara, "No, I'm not disappointed. Just surprised."

"Good!" she said. "Uncle Peter said you would be."

"Did he?" said I, with a small laugh that vowed vengeance.

She jerked her upper body toward the hallway impatiently. "Is Briley's or Papagozzi's within walking distance?"

"For Paul Bunyan, yes."

She laughed, a little too enthusiastically.

"Tara," I said (Tar-a, I pronounced it, as in the La Brea Pits, as instructed), "your uncle—"

"Tar-a?" she said.

"Yes."

"Tar-a?"

"Is that not your name?"

"Tare-a!"

"Tare-a?"

"Tare-a!"

"I was told it was Tar-a."

She giggled. "Uncle Peter strikes again!"

"Heh, heh," I said.

"Call it," she said, digging a hand into her jeans.

"Excuse me?"

"Call it. Heads, Briley's; tails, Papagozzi's."

"Huh?"

"If the nickel comes up heads, we go to Briley's. If it comes up tails, we go to Papagozzi's. You're a college professor?"

"Er," I said, in a sad attempt to buy the time to shuffle through the Rolodex of alternatives that were presenting themselves to me.

The mysterious telephone caller (the "friend") who expected to meet me at eight at Papagozzi's must know what I looked like — to go there in the company of another would undoubtedly put that "friend" off, and I might never discover what danger I was in until it was sloshing up over my forehead.

On the other hand, how coincidental that Peter should mention Papagozzi's as a possibility to his niece...was he involved in the "organization"? Was this their skillful way of insuring that I did *not* meet with the "friend"? Or was the "friend" a ruse on their part to get me to Papagozzi's? Toward what end? *Toward what end?*

I was being silly. There were a million possibilities, but by far the most likely of them was that I was turning into a delusional paranoiac. I had to get myself under control. I steeled my nerves and exerted what was left of my will. I shouldn't think about the future. Or even the past. I should immerse myself in the present. The immediate present.

I frowned. The immediately present question was, why was I even contemplating going out with this Tara Fury? Had I not told Peter "We'll see"? Since when did that mean, "Yes!"? What made me feel I had to accommodate this woman and her sadistic Torquemadan uncle?

"Tare-a," I said, "I have a lot of work to get done here. Honestly, I just don't have the time to go out tonight."

"We can order in," she said, without missing a beat. "You like pizza?"

"Tara, please — listen, your uncle may have misled you about my" — how should I phrase this? — "my desire for company this evening."

"How could he have misled me about your desire for company this evening?"

"He may have led you to believe I had any."

She eyeballed me. "You have none?"

"It's not you, Tara. I'm busy, is all."

"You're sure?"

"Yes."

She cast her eyes downward. The corners of her mouth followed soon after. "If you're sure," she muttered, slinking away.

It was the worst appeal for gentlemanly pity I have ever witnessed.

And the most successful.

"Tara," I said, "we'll take my car. Papagozzi's isn't far."

"Oh good!" she cheeped, clapping her hands together. "Uncle Peter said you were a pushover."

CHAPTER VIII
PAPAGOZZI'S

PAPAGOZZI'S WAS AN ODD PLACE. THE FOOD WAS SUPERB, BUT the lighting was so poor a bat would have had trouble navigating, and the booths were so private they could have storehoused plutonium; the route from the front entrance through the darkened labyrinth to our booth, deep beneath the surface of the earth, took the better part of five minutes. The maitre d', a tall, thin, serious individual, led us on this trek, but how he found his way without a torch in hand, I shall never know.

Having arrived at our booth, we settled into our seats. The maitre d' then reversed into the darkness with a bow of his head. I spread my napkin across my lap and took up the menu.

I knew I was ignoring Tara to some extent, but this date hadn't been my idea, and consequently I felt little responsibility for its achievements, or lack thereof. Conversation between us during the trip to the restaurant had consisted of Tara's retelling of the plane ride that had brought her to California — her first trip, apparently, on an airplane — during which not a single unusual thing had happened; but of course when you're riding a plane for the first time every little thing is unusual, and must be shared as if it were the golden tablets of Joseph Smith. Tara never noticed — or at least gave no indication of noticing — the glaze that draped over my gaze like creeping molasses, and I feared this was going to turn out to be a very long night indeed. Repeatedly I had insisted that I could only stay for an hour or so, but Tara, enthralled as she'd been by mild turbulence and the rigors of baggage check, had paid scant attention.

A waiter appeared, his skin a pale gray, providing him the appearance of a ghostly apparition emerging from the gloom. "Cocktail?" he asked in an ethereal whisper.

"Root beer for me, please," said Tara.

"Iced tea," I added.

"One iced tea, one root beer," the waiter wrote on his pad, sighing heavily, his tone dripping with world-weary sarcasm, as if his salary was dependent on commissions from sales of spirits. "As you wish." He spun about and threaded his way into the shadowy underworld.

Tara shrugged her shoulders, a gesture that said, Hey, it's California. What can you do?

I went back to the menu.

As we had made our stygian way to the booth I had done what little searching I could, given the inky blackness, a darkness not known since the first few verses of Genesis, but I had not seen any suspicious-looking characters — no trench coats, no felt hats with brims pulled low, no dangling cigarettes, no curious bulges just above the belt. The time was only 7:30, though — half an hour to go until the allotted time for my "friend" to make his (her?) appearance — and besides, in that light, Leopold and Lobe could have been sitting at the next booth and I'd have been none the wiser.

The waiter delivered our drinks, both in the same thick brown glasses.

"So tell me about yourself," said Tara.

We stared at one another for what didn't just seem like, but probably was, eternity.

"Well?" she prompted.

"Oh!" I said, realizing with a start that, almost uniquely among my dates, Tara had actually evinced an interest in me.

"You're a professor?"

"Yes," I answered.

"That's interesting. You must be very smart."

I thought of certain of my colleagues. "That doesn't necessarily follow," I said.

"It does in your case," she said. "You're very smart. I can tell."

I saw no reason to question her judgment.

She was nodding, agreeing with herself, then her gaze drifted lazily over my shoulder. As the only thing she could have seen over my shoulder was the railing atop the booth, I took this as a sign that her interest in me had reached a dead end.

I can't say why I said what I did next, except that it seemed like the thing to do at the time — I was only trying to get through the night with as little effort as possible. Given subsequent events, however, the sentence has taken on an import I could never have imagined, etching itself in my memory like a footprint on the moon.

"But enough about me. What about you?"

*   *   *

She began to discourse and didn't stop for a good half an hour. The waiter returned for our order six times — Tara hadn't decided on an entrée before beginning her deposition, and she refused to interrupt herself long enough to peruse the menu and finalize her selection. At first this troubled me, as I was far more concerned with eating than I was with hearing her personal history, but the more she talked, the more, despite myself, I became engrossed in her tale…like a soap opera you know is rotting your brain but can't help watching anyway.

I summarize, then, as she did not:

Tara Fury was born in Atlanta, into a proud southern clan which, family tradition taught, her uncle's (Peter's) father had rebelled against and offshot from when his mother — who would be Peter's grandmother and Tara's great-grandmother — denied Peter's father's request to join what Peter's grandmother called "Roosevelt's Army" and fight the Nazis, whom Peter's grandmother called "misunderstood."

Peter's father ran off and joined up anyway, prompting Peter's grandmother to disown him, thereby creating a western wing of the Cranston family; a western wing whom in the eyes of their eastern relatives could never quite measure up, even after Peter's grandmother passed on and family leadership fell to Peter's cousin Theodore, whom Tara referred to as "a nice man" but who, out of loyalty to his dead mother's memory, rejected his disinherited brother's proposal for reunification, which included a generous full apology...I'm sounding like Emily Brontë, but this isn't my story, so you can't blame me.

The latest news from the Cranston clan was that Tara's generation was making great strides in binding up the ancient wounds. The staunchest supporter of these efforts among the *Ancien Régime* was none other than good old Uncle Peter. He was Tara's favorite, and this visit of hers to California was a bold move on her part to further the cause of ultimate reconciliation. Some in the eastern wing would interpret it as a thumbed nose, she said, but she hoped it might also give them pause to reflect and reconsider their position.

If they're anything like you, I thought, *it'll take a lot more than that to make them pause.*

Slurping the foam from the top of her root beer, she stated loftily, but without arrogance, "My goal in life is to reunite the two warring factions. I would like to be remembered as the Abraham Lincoln of the Cranston family."

The upper half of my face was caught off-guard by the absurdity of this declaration, which resulted in my eyebrows rising to previously unexplored heights, but the lower half of my face was caught up in an instinctual tendering of encouragement to this brave girl going about her brave business, which resulted in a warped and unnatural smile. I must have looked like a living Picasso, but Tara only appeared to perceive, and pay heed to, the smile, which she returned.

Then she said, unexpectedly, "What's *your* family like?"

She'd caught me off-guard a second time. In-between her rambling, discursive monologues, she needed to give her larynx a break, it seemed, and her method of doing so was to throw me a conversational bone. This particular bone, I wished she hadn't picked — I loved my family, Lord knows, but they weren't a subject I'd have brought up on a first date. Probably not even on a fifty-first date. To them Shakespeare was something the natives did just before they attacked.

But, again, this was not a thing a person says out loud. I mulled over a more respectable answer, reaching down to the table and picking up a drink without even looking at it. I swallowed a quick gulp and tasted root beer.

"Oh, sorry—" I set the drink back down. "That's yours, not mine."

Tara smiled. "Looks like your family is a source of discombobulation."

I snorted, for this was something of an understatement.

She leaned forward. "Are you afraid to talk about your family?"

"No, no," I said. "They're just — nothing special. —I mean, they're special to me, but they're not extraordinary in any way."

I chanced to glance at my watch. It was after 8. My "friend" might be watching us even as we spoke. I made a halfhearted attempt to search the booths around us, but I needed a klieg light, and as it happened I'd left mine at home.

"Where do they live?"

"Huh?"

"Your parents," said Tara. "Where do they live?"

"Oh. Kansas."

"Any brothers, sisters?"

"No. I'm an only child."

"I have two sisters. We fight like the dickens. Cain, Abel, and Seth, they call us. I'm Seth—"

And with that, she launched into rambling, discursive monologue #3. I don't recall much of it, except that, obviously, it had to do with her and her sisters. I was distracted by thoughts of the "friend" — was he watching me even now? What did he want to tell me? What danger was I in? Should I excuse myself to get up and walk around, so he'd have a chance to contact me?

In due course, however, I was distracted by something else.

The poison took effect.

My head fell to the table.

CHAPTER IX
POISONED

I AM A VORACIOUS CONSUMER OF BOOKS, BUT NOT IN ANY OF MY reading have I come across a first-hand account of what it is like to be poisoned. There's no dearth of first-hand accounts of what it is like to be the poison*er*: read any British mystery. But the converse, to be the poison*ed*? The world could do with a good poisoned narrative.

But this is not it. My memory of this poisoning is — my experience of this poisoning was — limited to a lapse from awareness into a deep slumber. Perhaps that's all there is to most poisonings, I don't know. But it's not an especially dramatic memory of what was, after all, a fairly dramatic event — some people may get poisoned every day, but I try to limit it to once a lifetime, if even that.

From that deep slumber I awoke with a pain that throbbed and pounded and pushed at the envelope of my skull, the Chuck Yeager of headaches. My vision was blurry. My movements were ponderous. My speech, when it came, was incomprehensible even to me.

"Take it easy," said a soothing female voice.

My head turned heavily toward its source.

Its source was a pretty young girl in a nurse's uniform.

Oh, I'm in a hospital.

This thought rammed into my cerebrum — I came awake so fully and completely that for a brief instant I could swear I understood the secret of creation. It was but an instant, though, and I have not been able to recollect any of it. (I remember the little things, but forget the Nobel Prize material.)

I was in a hospital. Either that, or this girl had extraordinarily bad taste in decorating. Gray wells, black-and-white checkered tile floor, two metal wire beds, a window with, from my vantage point, a vista of the morning sky — it was morning? — and a television perched on a bar about a foot short of the ceiling that one would have to be sitting on the ceiling to be able to view without the aid of a chiropractor.

Yes, this was a hospital, all right.

Why was I in the hospital?

Where was Tara?

"You may be suffering from a slight disorientation," said the nurse.

Slight?

"You're in Perpetual Hospital, third floor, Room 306. The antidote has taken care of the poison, but your body has been through a trauma."

"Poi...poison?"

My words sent an echo reverberating throughout my bones, as if I'd been standing too close to the tower bell in the church courtyard.

"Yes," confirmed the nurse. "In your drink."

"My...date..." I considered this for a second. "I mean, my companion?"

"Companion?" She gave me a look that conveyed the message that if my "companion" was male, she was not the sort of person who would condemn me for my choice of lifestyle, and there was no call for me to go covering it up because of my own homophobiaphobia. "I'll check for you," she said. "What's the name?"

"Tara."

She registered this exclusively-female name with a downward turn of her lips. Apparently she'd been looking forward to showing off her broadmindedness. "Last name?"

"Fury."

"I'll check. Don't move about, now. Rest easy."

I leaned back on my pillow as she removed the IV needle from my arm and inserted a fresh one. She walked out of the room with that purposeful stride I imagine must be the first prerequisite for a nursing certificate.

Poisoned. Me, Miles Hudson, *poisoned.* Why? Who? Dr. Humphreys? The organization? The "friend"? Tara? Peter?

It hurt to think about it. It hurt to think about anything.

I looked at my body, laid out on the bed, decked out in a white smock. I looked at the intravenous tube, plugged into my vein. I followed the tube as it ran up my shoulder, under the bedsheets, and on up to the bag of clear liquid that dripped, dripped...but it *wasn't* dripping.

Had the nurse made a mistake? Her appearance had been so professional. Possibly this was a new type of IV, that did not drip?

I touched the needle, and felt a sharp sting. It was stuck into my vein, no doubt of that, leisurely feeding a pinkish fluid into my bloodstream.

Synapses fired. The pieces of the puzzle swirled in my mind and came together to form a covered bridge in Vermont.

A pinkish fluid was leisurely flooding into my bloodstream — a pinkish fluid that, I would bet, was odorless and wouldn't be noticed when poured into iced tea!

I lifted the sheets.

Another plastic bag was there, filled with pink fluid, topped with a small, noiseless pump that was even now pushing the fluid into my bloodstream—

I tore the needle from my arm, and flung it, and its tube, and its plastic baggie reservoir of poison, out the window.

"Ow!" yipped a squeaky voice. "Mommy!"

But I couldn't have cared less. How much of a dose had I received? Enough to kill me? They'd obviously underestimated my immune system last night — surely they'd upped the dosage for the second round!

A short, thin man ambled into the room.

"'Morning, Dr. Hudson," he said. "How are we?" His voice and manner were exceedingly obsequious, like a teenager asking his father for the car keys.

I opened my mouth as the man moved to one side, revealing Tara standing behind him. She ran to me and put her arms around me and gave me a hug that proved two things. One, her drink had not been poisoned, or, if it had, had caused her no lasting repercussions. Two, mine had.

"Miles, Miles," she cooed, showering my face with undelicate kisses.

"Don't mean to intrude," said the short man, intruding most welcomely. "Have a couple questions to ask, then I'll be outta your hair."

"Oh!" I said, slapping my forehead against Tara's as I leaned up in the bed, "the nurse! The *nurse!* She tried to poison me again! You can still catch her! Medium height, brown eyes, brown hair—"

"Holy cow!" said the short man. He pointed at Tara. "The woman in the elevator!"

"That's right!" said Tara.

"Ahhhhhhh!" said the short thin man as he rushed from the room.

"Get a doctor!" I implored Tara.

But just then another nurse entered. I shrank away from her. "Ahhhhhhh!" I cried, which seemed to be the order of the day.

"It's okay, Miles," said Tara. "She's your real nurse."

This legitimate nurse held up the empty poison baggie, its tubes trailing to the floor.

"Dr. Hudson," she said sternly, "this is hospital property. We have traced it to your window. We do not condone this sort of irresponsibility, Dr. Hudson. You frightened a little boy right back into intensive care, and you also ruined his teddy bear."

"I was being *poisoned!*"

"That's no excuse, Dr. Hudson."

"Did you do that, Miles?" asked Tara.

"Call the doctor!" I croaked.

"I most certainly *will* call the doctor," said the nurse. "And I most certainly *will* inform him of this little incident, and I most certainly *will* suggest that we discharge you immediately!"

"That wasn't very considerate, Miles," said Tara.

"We could be *sued*, Dr. Hudson. But that thought never crossed your mind, did it?"

The short thin man reappeared. "My men are searching the premises. If she's still in the building we'll find her. If she isn't we won't."

"Who's that you're looking for?" asked the nurse.

I answered, "Brown eyes, brown hair, tremendously winning attitude toward her patients. Maybe you remember her from nursing school."

"Doc's on his way," said the short man.

"Just who are you, anyhow?" I asked him, finally realizing that there was a man in my hospital room and also that I had no idea who he was.

His put his hands on his hips, but the effect was less Superman and more Clark Kent. "I am Chief Detective Superintendent Chauncey," said he. "County of Constant."

My response was: "Are you."

"Yes, I am," he said. He came to stand directly beside the bed, addressing me with grave significance. "Dr. Hudson, there have been two attempts on your life within the past twelve hours. You're lucky to be alive. The people behind these attempts are ruthless — determined — and highly organized."

Organized?

Now where had I heard that before?

*   *   *

I was released from the hospital three hours later by Dr. Utley, a man whose field of vision appeared confined to his metallic chart.

"Tests are negative," he said authoritatively, and slapped the chart shut with such finality that I was certain I would never be sick again. "Fast-acting stuff, but the carbonation in the soft drink diluted the poison. You can go anytime."

"Thank you, Doctor," I said.

But he had already quit the room, off to another chart. I mean patient.

The imposter nurse had not been found. No one remembered seeing her in the hospital before — and a similar story was told regarding the waiter at Papagozzi's.

"Any reason anybody'd want to kill you?" Chauncey asked me.

"Are you implying there might be a reason that's good enough?"

"No, no, goodness, no, Dr. Hudson. Looking for leads, that's all. Somebody wants you dead. No idea who?"

I had an excellent idea who. The organized organization to which I was codename "Fish."

"No idea at all," I said to Chauncey.

"Hmm," he said. "We're a small force here in Constant, not a lot of manpower. But in a matter like this we can spare a man for your protection, if you want him."

"'If I want him'?"

"I won't force him on you."

"Of course I want him! My life is in danger! Of course I want protection!"

"Fine, fine. I'll assign Officer Gerald to your case. He's not our best man, but he's up there, right up there."

"...?" I didn't say.

"He'll do good by you, Dr. Hudson. You have my word on it."

The Chief Detective Superintendent smiled benignly, shook my hand, and trundled out the door.

I looked at Tara. "I haven't felt this confident since my first day of high school."

"Miles — they've tried to kill you twice already, and both times you've foiled them. If they try a third time, you'll foil them again. If they try a fourth time, you'll foil them! They can try till Doomsday, you'll foil them every time! —Miles? Miles?"

I was staring straight ahead — not because of what Tara had just said, though that was more than sufficient cause — but because of what Dr. Utley had said, a statement that had taken its own sweet time to register at the overcrowded hotel that passed for my brain.

"Tara—"

"Yes, Miles?"

"What the doctor said — the *carbonation* diluted the poison?"

"Yeah, that's what he said. Lucky for you!"

"Tara — iced tea isn't carbonated."

She goggled at me uncomprehendingly.

"Iced tea isn't carbonated," I repeated. "But *root beer* is."

Her expression did not change.

"I drank most of my tea, Tara. It couldn't have been poisoned, or I'd be dead right now. The doctor said the stuff was fast-acting…when I took that drink of your root beer, the poison hit me almost immediately. —But why didn't it hit *you?*"

Her expression changed, considerably. "I didn't — I didn't drink any of it, Miles," she stammered. "I was too busy telling you about my family. I just…slurped the foam…"

I grabbed her arms. "Tara — listen to me. The waiter did the poisoning, and he knew whose drink was whose. You see? I poisoned myself by mistake — but the waiter meant the poison *for you!*"

CHAPTER X
GYPSY

"POISON!" CRIED PETER. "IT'S *MEDIEVAL!*"

Peter's presence was one surprise awaiting me at my apartment. The other was an engraved invitation from Dr. Franklin Allen Humphreys to "Eighteen Holes of Gala Golf" at Everlasting House.

"Yet another coincidence..." I muttered, fingering the silky stationery.

"What coincidence is that?" asked Peter.

"Flynn's been dying to play that course. He's been pressuring me to put in a request."

"You're on Humphreys' good side, that's plain. I've never been asked to play there." Peter sniffed.

"Question is, do I take the good Dean up on his offer?"

"I'm mystified," said Tara. "Poison. Me. Who could do such a thing? To me, of all people! I wouldn't hurt a flea! Unless it was carrying some awful disease."

"Let's not go overboard, Tara," said Peter. "I'm not the least bit convinced you were the intended victim. Remember that student of yours, Miles? You gave her a D in 'Renaissance and Reformation'? She said she'd get back at you if it was the last thing she ever did?"

"Ex-students don't attempt to murder their professors, Peter." I reconsidered the blanketness of this statement. "Well, maybe yours do, but mine don't."

"She was a frail old woman…like a gypsy. I remember she threatened you in public."

"With a bad case of warts, not poisoning. Besides which, I was poisoned by a man."

"Last night you were — but in the hospital? The waiter could have been the old woman's accomplice, and when he failed, she tried to finish the job herself!"

"The nurse was a young girl, Peter. That gypsy was an eyewitness to Gettysburg. —Please, no more speculation. I'm trying to think this through logically and rationally. Your grassy knoll/second shooter theories aren't helping any."

"I'm only saying, you should tell the police to look on the outskirts of town," Peter advised. "That's where they set up camp, as a rule."

*   *   *

Actually, I had already thought it through. At first it was quite puzzling, but once I decided that Tara was the intended victim of the first poisoning, the only theory that fit the facts was that the second poisoning was meant to keep me from realizing that Tara was the intended victim of the first poisoning. I was easy prey, there on the hospital bed, and without my warning to Tara, she'd have been easy prey, as well.

I was also convinced that nothing that had occurred in the last two days had occurred in and of itself — some thread ran through it all, some linkage and bond, that I could not perceive.

Tara was definitely in danger. She could think of no possible reason why. Knowing her as little as I did, I could think of no possible reason why, either — save one of her relatives objecting to her "overture" to the western wing of the Cranston family. But that was hardly worth killing her for, was it? As opposed to having to listen to her explain the whole thing again, which *might* be worth killing her for.

I was definitely in danger, as well — on two fronts, I hypothesized. Firstly for the reason outlined above, and now that I had realized the truth and warned Tara, that danger might have passed for me. Secondly for the reason the "friend," from whom I'd heard nothing more, presumably would have divulged if I had met him (or her) at Papagozzi's...if the "friend" weren't a crank caller with a Goebbels-like sense of humor.

Then, to top it off, there was Humphreys' offer of a round of golf. To accept the offer was to walk knowingly into what was likely a trap. Set against this, though, were three essentials in my favor. I would have Flynn along (though whether he would be a help or a hindrance was, I had to admit, an open question). I could contact Chauncey, and have him storm the place if Flynn and I were so much as five minutes behind schedule at the end of the round. And lastly, Dr. Humphreys, deranged Dr. Humphreys, might possibly let something slip in the course of four hours, some clue to reveal that invisible connecting thread.

On the whole, I decided that "Eighteen Holes of Gala Golf" was not such a bad idea after all.

Yet another example in the annals of decision-making of the category *Lousy*.

*   *   *

The telephone rang.

"Hello?" I said into the mouthpiece.

"Hi, Dr. Hudson, Officer Gerald here. I've taken up a position in an adjoining apartment, and I am, as we speak, installing elaborate listening and recording equipment. I should be finished by nightfall."

"Let's hope they hold off until then," I said.

"Yes, let's!" said Officer Gerald, and laughed.

I glared at him, though he was not there. "Which apartment are you in?"

"I'd rather not say."

"Do you know which apartment *I'm* in?"

"That's not amusing, Dr. Hudson."

"I'm playing golf this afternoon. Will that be a problem?"

"Yes, it will. I'd rather you canceled."

"Then I shall go most joyfully."

"I can't help you if you won't cooperate, Dr. Hudson."

"Do you play golf, Officer?"

"My handicap is five."

"You could join us."

"I am supposed to be undercover. I lose a surprising amount of my effectiveness if the other side discovers I exist."

"Truly, a distressing prospect."

"Where are you playing golf?"

"Everlasting House."

"I'm almost tempted to change my answer."

"I'm almost tempted to withdraw my invitation."

"Dr. Hudson. I am the one man who stands between you and the persons who would like you dead. It may be unwise to antagonize me."

"I see your point, Officer Gerald."

"Have a good game, Dr. Hudson."

I rang off and looked at Peter. "Constant's finest. I should make certain my will is in order."

The phone buzzed again.

"Hello?"

"Old hog!"

"Hi, Flynn."

"Top o' the mornin'! You speak to Humphreys?"

"No, but I did receive in this morning's mail an invitation to play a round at Everlasting House this very afternoon."

I held the phone away from my ear.

"I'll pick you up at noon."

I held it further away.

"Goodbye, Flynn."

*   *   *

To fill the rest of the morning, I again questioned Tara regarding potential reasons why an unknown somebody, or somebodies, might want to poison her. She stared out the window for a considerable while before she said, "I guess I've made enemies here and there — I mean, who hasn't? — but geez, I can't think of *one* person I've ticked off enough to want to kill me. I may have ticked off one or two enough to want me dead, but that's a far cry from actually doing something about it."

"The feud in your family? No hard feelings there?"

"Plenty of hard feelings, believe me. But they're *family*. They may hate me, but they're not going to kill me, for heaven's sake."

Peter was gaping at his niece. "You told Miles about the family?"

"Yes, I did."

"Why in the world would you do a thing like that?"

"I was sharing. Opening up."

"It was your *first* date! Why not just hand over your ATM card and your PIN code and be done with it?"

"Uncle Peter, so what if he knows about the family feud? It's not a secret."

"It's none of his business! One date and you're spilling family confidences? Was this *pillow talk*, perhaps?"

"Uncle Peter! How could we have slept together? He got poisoned."

I determined that this was my moment to step in. "Maybe we're overlooking an alternate motive. Maybe they were striking at Tara to get to you, Peter."

They both gaped at me. This was obviously not an alternative either had considered, and the reason they had not considered it was that it was moronic.

"You're not serious," said Peter. "If they wanted to 'get to me,' why wouldn't they simply poison *my* root beer?"

"You don't drink root beer, Uncle Peter."

"I know it sounds ridiculous," I said, "but everything about this situation sounds ridiculous. I'm only trying to cover all the bases."

"You do that when you hit a home run, Miles, and that theory is not a home run. It's more like a weak ground ball to the pitcher."

"It's no worse than your deranged gypsy with a grudge theory."

"I'm telling you, listen for the squeezeboxes! They'll lead you right to her!"

I looked at my watch. Noon was nearing.

"All right. I have to go. You and Tara stay here. Don't leave. Don't set foot outside this apartment. If we're not back here by four-thirty, call Gerald, he must be in 35, next door. If you can't get him, call Chauncey — but you'd better not reach him, because he'd better be with the SWAT Team that's coming in after us."

"Miles," said Peter, "you're being paranoid. Everlasting House is better-guarded than Fort Knox. They'll be all over that gypsy before she's ten feet on the grounds."

CHAPTER XI
GOPHERS

WE WERE DRIVEN FROM EVERLASTING HOUSE TO THE FIRST TEE BY Jenkins, in a 1932 Bentley. Dr. Humphreys, bright and cheery and talkative, sat with us in the Batcavernous back seat. The Bentley, he explained, was a present to his family from Lord Mountbatten, for services rendered during his time in China. The road we traveled, Dr. Humphreys explained, was over a century old. The elms and willows we passed, he explained, were seeded by Roderick Blanding himself. The gardener, he explained, was an ex-groundskeeper for Ebbets Field who'd retired in disgust when the wrecking ball fell. The golf course's architect, he explained, was a protégé of Bobby Jones who'd come to California after his wife had run off with his mistress.* The golf course's grass, Dr. Humphreys explained,

---

* Dr. Humphreys breezed through these explanations like a guilty husband breezing from "I have to work late again" to "Here's that pearl necklace you've been eyeing, sweetheart." Later I did some research and discovered that the golf course architect in question, Timothy Winert, had been married for forty years before taking up with a 23-year old lady golfer just prior to World War II. Once the war began, Winert was called to Washington on "top-secret" business and was away for eight months. He returned in the summer of 1942 and immediately knew he was in trouble when he read the nameplate on his mailbox: "Mrs. & Mrs. Angela Winert." Winert lost everything in the ensuing divorce, but made a second fortune by rededicating himself to his craft — the Course at Everlasting House being the capstone of his comeback. Shortly after completing

was a hybrid blade that required less water to thrive than did most cacti.

During these explanations my eyes never left their explainer. I had never seen Dr. Humphreys this carefree — did he not know, had he not been told, of the organization's plans for me? For Tara? If he did know, he was a fantastic actor. Or a fantastic sociopath.

"Ah," he said as the scenery surrounding us slowed, "we've arrived."

Jenkins held open the door for us. Dr. Humphreys was smart and dapper in a tweed mackintosh. I was modernly attired, in a cottony way. Flynn had us both beat, though, in his eight-quarter cap, gray knickers, and blue-and-yellow argyle socks.

"Jenkins will be caddying for me today," said the Dean. He pointed at the clubhouse, fifty yards or so from the vehicle. Five young men, by their appearance ranging in age from twelve to nineteen, stood in a row. "Our House caddies, if you care to avail yourselves."

"No, thank you," said Flynn, hauling his clubs from the trunk.

"Miles?"

Every one of those young people possessed the off-putting stare of the self-assured. Any one of them could have easily outshot me, and knew it.

"I'll pass," I said.

"A cart?" asked Dr. Humphreys. "It can be a long eighteen holes."

---

the course, however, his new mistress ran off with his son. Winert was distraught, but soon fell in love again, with his daughter's husband. He was happy for a time, until his son ran off with his daughter, at which point he gave it all up and hung himself.

"No, thank you," said Flynn, already teed up and taking practice swings.

"A purist, eh?" Dr. Humphreys nodded appreciatively. "Very well, our first hole is a 535-yard par five, dogleg left. You want to place your first shot to the right of that bunker there, that'll give you a good chance to reach the green in two."

Flynn's club struck his ball at the exact instant Dr. Humphreys completed his narration.

There was a moment of silence.

"Where'd you go?" I asked.

"I lost sight of it," said Dr. Humphreys. "It looked left, initially."

Flynn was pulling up his tee. "I'm in the eighteenth fairway," he said merrily. He slid his driver into its allotted corner of his bag. "Who's next?"

I had not played with Flynn before, golf not having interested him in the slightest before a few weeks prior to this; but thanks to his fevered devotion, I expected his game to be far better than, from this first shot, I judged it to be. Still, everyone makes a bad shot now and then. And Flynn was certainly keyed up to be playing, at long last, the course of his dreams — no surprise that his nerves might get the better of him.

"Miles." Dr. Humphreys gestured toward the tee.

When I was in college I played golf regularly, but since then I had played, at best, once or twice a year. My game was average, and never seemed subject to the wild variations that most people's games suffer. I addressed the ball and hit it short, and none too straight. Par for the course, so to speak, for my golf game.

"Jenkins, perhaps you'd best go with Miles and help him find his ball," suggested Dr. Humphreys.

"Yes, Jenkins, perhaps you'd best," I mumbled, squinting at the broad fairway.

Dr. Humphreys studied the menagerie of club heads protruding from his bag. "Let's see, Jenkins…a driver?"

"This hole would seem to call for a driver, yes, sir."

Dr. Humphreys blasted the ball through the air, high and straight and far.

"We're off!" he proclaimed with ebullience.

He and Flynn marched from the tee down the sloping bank. I trudged along after them, Jenkins beside me. About twenty feet beyond the tee, we split into three directions. Dr. Humphreys continued forward, Flynn pared off to the left, I pared off to the right. From above, we must have looked like a trio of Navy jets.

My ball had landed in a broad patch of heavy scrub where the grass was at least a foot high, in places as much as three. I was about to tell Jenkins that I would declare a lost ball and take a drop when I noticed a glistening white circle.

"Difficult shot, sir," said Jenkins.

"Thank you for pointing that out. Five iron, you think?"

"To be candid, sir, I am not convinced it matters."

I took a five iron. The bottom third of the club disappeared in the tangled scrub. I swung the club head back and down. It was like swinging through water, but I finished with a smooth follow-through. I was so mightily impressed with my swing that I forgot to watch the ball. I looked at Jenkins. It may have been the light passing through the heavy foliage overhead, but I thought I saw incredulity stamped on his face.

"Fine shot!" I heard Flynn shout.

"Where'd I go?" I asked Jenkins.

"You are on the green, sir. I would estimate thirty feet from the cup."

"You're kidding."

"No, sir. I would not find that funny, sir."

"Well!" I said.

"Yes, sir."

Dr. Humphreys did not waste much time hitting his second shot. It landed ten or fifteen yards short, but rolled right up to the edge of the green. Jenkins estimated he would have a thirty-five foot eagle putt.

Flynn, however, was having his troubles. He was quite a distance away, but I saw him take four different swings — literally, as in four different *motions* — at four different locations. Finally I saw his ball shoot through a tall tree which, luckily, killed much of its momentum; the ball dropped into a green-side bunker.

As we walked up to the green, though, he did not seem overly concerned. He took a wedge and, after elaborate preparations, swiped at the ball. All I saw was a white blur, then Jenkins' arm flashing like lightning, and then the ball rolling on the green, inches from the cup…

But the ball was rolling *toward* Flynn. Either he had put an ungodly amount of backspin on it, or Jenkins had caught it and tossed it back toward the cup.

"Am I out?" asked Dr. Humphreys. His was a long uphill putt breaking sharply from his left to right. He lined up around twelve inches above the hole.

"You're not playing enough break," commented Flynn.

"Oh?" said the Dean. He frowned, and after a moment of reconsideration, realigned his stance so that he was lined up around sixteen inches above the hole. He brought the putter back…swept it forward…his ball spun across the green, up the slope, flitting along the break…and stopped four inches above the hole.

"Greens are fast," was Flynn's epitaph on this eagle attempt. "When was the last time you watered?"

My ball lay, as Jenkins had predicted, thirty feet away. I had the same slope Dr. Humphreys had had to deal with, but mine ran right-to-left. I did not look at Flynn at any time until the ball was well on its way.

It came closer than the Dean's, but still missed.

"Greens are fast," repeated Flynn, and promptly skipped his three-inch putt six feet past the hole. By an act of providence his second putt caught the far edge of the cup, and after a few heart-stopping revolutions about the lip, plunked in.

Dr. Humphreys and I putted out, both of us scoring birdies. Flynn had scored — I'm afraid there is no actual word for what Flynn had scored. I was charitable and put down a six on the scorecard.

*   *   *

So it continued. Flynn's play was abominable, but it didn't faze him in the least — he had, seemingly, achieved the amateur golfer's dream of disregarding the score he was posting and playing the game purely for the joy of it. Dr. Humphreys was playing a consistent round. I was making dreadful shots and making up for them with unbelievable recoveries. Or making unbelievable shots and ruining them with dreadful second shots. In short, my game was subject to the same wild variations as most peoples'. The end result was that Dr. Humphreys and I were neck-and-neck. Flynn was…well, no adjective applies, or, should I say, suffices.

*   *   *

I struggled to broach the subject of the organization with the good Dean as we traipsed down the second, third, fourth, and fifth fairways. But before I could question Dr. Humphreys I had to answer a question I had asked myself, which was, How do I question Dr. Humphreys? How do I broach the subject?

Can I offer you a glass of root beer, Dr. Humphreys?

Why don't you do your own dirty work, you psychotic murderer?

Do you see this two wood? Do you know what I'd like to do with it?

No need for formality, Franky. Call me by my old college moniker: Fish.

None of these quite passed muster. None of these, frankly, would have passed a little old lady in the slow lane. Thus it happened that I did not broach the subject of the organization.

Nor did Dr. Humphreys let slide from his lips any remarks other than his continuing travelogue of the Course at Everlasting House. Just as with everything when it came to Dr. Humphreys' explanations, it seemed that each tree, each shrub, each bunker, each fairway, each green, had some oblique connection to a historical personage. The pair of red men's tee markers on the fourth hole, for instance, had once served as champagne buckets for Bertie, Prince of Wales. Never mind the ©1973 stamped on the side.

We came to the sixth hole.

Par four, a narrow straightaway demarked by trees. To hit anywhere but straight down the fairway was to double-bogey the hole.

Flynn's ball bounded off at nearly a right angle to us, and Dr. Humphreys and I each hit decent shots that landed within a few feet of each other.

"Seven iron, eh?" he said, as I pulled an eight from my bag.

"Of course," I said.

His second shot sailed over the green.

I stood over my ball. I looked at the flag, back at the ball. My muscles tensed, preparing for the backswing—

Pfut.

Pfut.

Pfut.

A clump of dirt by my foot lifted into the air and disintegrated.

A stick four feet from my foot splintered into pulp.

A pine cone on a nearby tree exploded.

I frowned and looked at Dr. Humphreys. "What was that?"

"What was what, Miles?"

"The dirt there, and that stick, and the pine cone..."

He walked over and poked at the clump with his club. "Gophers," he said conclusively. "They're a recurring problem, I'm afraid."

"Gophers? Up in a tree?"

"No, Miles. Under the ground. That's where they live, you know. They dig tunnels, burrow caves. Ingenious little critters, but destructive as all get-out."

My brow must have looked like corrugated tin. But this was Dr. Humphreys, so I knew better than to press the issue.

I re-approached the ball, my step wary, but once in position, I swung in a hurry. The ball arced into the air and fell gently onto the green with a feather-soft kerplunk.

"That was a seven iron?" queried Dr. Humphreys, scowling.

"Of course," I replied.

We finished the sixth hole without further incident, and the seventh, as well. On the eighth, however, as I was putting, I felt something nick my ear.

Pfut.

"There it was again!" I cried.

"There *what* was?"

"The *noise!*"

Pfut.

The flagstick creaked. The top half toppled to the green.

"*That* noise?" asked Flynn.

"Yes!"

Dr. Humphreys cradled the broken stick in his arms, his eyes inspecting the ragged tear that had separated it from its bottom half. "Curse those creatures..."

"It's *not* gophers!" I blurted. "They'd have to be five feet tall!"

"Anyone who's been around a golf course recognizes the sound of a gopher gnawing," Dr. Humphreys informed me in a patronizing tone.

"I don't see any teeth marks," I said, analyzing the two halves of the flagstick. "And since when do gophers gnaw on *graphite?*"

"Miles, I've been playing this course for going on thirty years. If a gopher will gnaw through a golf cart tire, as I once saw one do, then a gopher will surely gnaw through a flagstick, and I don't care if it's made of titanium steel."

I didn't accept this explanation for a second, but again, with Dr. Humphreys, pressing the issue was pointless. I may as well have started an argument with my own shoelaces.

I was last to hit on the ninth. The answer struck me as I was bringing back my driver. The club slipped from my hands and spun cartwheels through the morning air until it slapped back to earth farther from the tee than most of the balls it had been used to drive.

"*Miles!*" said an awestruck Flynn. "That was *Olympic!*"

"That's not a physical problem," said Dr. Humphreys. "That's a mental problem. Lack of concentration."

I was not inclined to argue with him, particularly as he was right. I had lost my concentration. Because it had struck me that *pfut* was rather like the sound made by a silenced weapon.

A silenced rifle.

Such as that used by, say, for instance, to take a random example, a sniper.

Those childhood hours spent watching television certainly were coming in handy.

Someone was shooting at me.

Someone was shooting at me!

"*Bullets!*" I shrieked.

"Bullets?" said Flynn.

"Bullets?" said Dr. Humphreys.

"Someone is *shooting* at me!"

Pfut.

Pfut.

Pfut.

Pfut.

Pfut.

"Gophers, gophers, everywhere!" yelped Dr. Humphreys. "Won't be a flagstick left standing!"

"Bullets, *bullets*, everywhere!" I shouted. I turned him bodily to the west. "*There!*" I pointed. "See the glint off the telescopic sight?"

"A gopher's *eyes*, Miles."

"Up in a *tree?*"

"They are ingenious critters."

I pulled a three wood from my bag and dropped five balls on the ground. Not bothering to take aim, I smashed one Titleist after another toward the treed rifleman. The first three sailed past, but the fourth struck home. A green-garbed form tumbled from the tree.

"My word!" said Dr. Humphreys. "That's not a gopher!"

"He's been firing at me since the sixth hole!"

"But why would he be firing at you since the sixth hole?"

I took a deep breath, and peered at Dr. Humphreys. "You knew nothing of this, did you? Nothing at all."

"I'm confused, Miles. A sniper? Here? This isn't Beirut, this is the Course at Everlasting House!"

I spun to face the fairway. I bellowed, "If there be other assassins lying in wait, know this: I have a large supply of balls, and from all evidence I'm a better marksman than any of you!"

My words echoed across the course. The only reply was an eerie, unnatural silence.

I turned to Dr. Humphreys and growled savagely, *"Let's finish the round."*

*   *   *

I was in an excellent mood when we returned to my apartment, and not merely because I had shot a 75, two under my previous eighteen-hole record (the knowledge that a high-powered firearm had been trained on me had elevated my game to stratospheric heights), but because Dr. Humphreys' name had been cleared. His instructions, no doubt, had merely been to get me out on the golf course — he had not been told of the snipers. He was, indeed, a low man on the organization's totem pole.

"4:18!" exclaimed Peter. "Twelve minutes early!"

Tara leapt into my arms, and gave me another of her bearish hugs. The girl was stronger than she looked. The girl was stronger than John Wayne looked.

"I was so worried!" she said, drawing back and drilling her eyes into mine. "Are you okay?"

"I'm fine. Shot a 75. How are you?"

"We're doing well," said Peter. "Though we've been bored out of our skulls, passing an absolutely monotonous afternoon. What did you shoot?" he asked Flynn.

Flynn smiled beatifically. "Doesn't matter. Any day spent golfing is a day closer to heaven."

The telephone rang.

"Hello?"

"Dr. Hudson."

"Officer Gerald, how nice to hear from you."

"I take it you made it back safely."

"An astute observation, Officer."

"I am famed for such, Dr. Hudson. Any…untoward… situations arise during your afternoon?"

"Untoward?"

"For example a poisoning, Dr. Hudson."

"No, Officer. No untoward situations. It was a pleasant afternoon of fun and games."

"I am sorry to hear that, Dr. Hudson."

"You are?"

"You weren't going to tell me about the gunmen? You weren't going to tell me how they fired approximately a dozen rounds at you? You do not consider that an *untoward* situation?"

"You — were there, Officer Gerald?"

"I was, Dr. Hudson. For your sake I was knocked from a tree by a dimpled ball that to my eyes resembled Halley's Comet, hammering toward a spot located approximately halfway up and halfway down my torso, if you'll pardon my French. I should think that this excruciating act of sacrifice ought to demonstrate to you that you can trust me."

"That was *you* in the tree?"

"Yes, Dr. Hudson. I have the swelling to prove it. I may have to sleep standing up tonight."

"Why didn't you stop the snipers, for God's—"

"I was about to, when you felled me."

"They'd been shooting at me for fifteen minutes! It took you all that time to figure out what the *pfut pfut pfut* was?"

"We lived next to a golf course when I was growing up, Dr. Hudson. I thought it was gophers."

Chapter XII
STRANGER IN THE NIGHT

Tara suggested that she and Peter remain at my apartment for the night. Peter was less than elated about the idea, the riflemen having obliterated his gypsy theory and persuaded him that being in my vicinity was bound to have an adverse effect on his health. But his niece shifted each of her one hundred pounds toward her backside, implanting herself in my recliner as solidly as an oak in bedrock, and sat there with her arms crossed. The battle between Peter's desire to be a living uncle and Peter's desire to be a chivalrous uncle played out on the canvas of his face, and, in the end, he went with the option least likely to cause a big scene.

Flynn, for whom big scenes are manna from heaven, remained at the apartment as well.

Around eight o'clock, Peter broke out a bottle of my best champagne. By which I mean, he broke out my *only* bottle of champagne, which had cost me a whopping $20 at the supermarket. I kept it in the refrigerator for those moments, few and far between, when I had something to celebrate. The fact that it had been sitting in the refrigerator for six months and was still unopened speaks to the questions of how few and how far between.

"Hey, big spender!" said Tara, because I'd forgotten to remove the price tag. "Spend a little time with me!"

"Yes, that's very funny," I said. "I was saving that for a special occasion—"

"From the looks of things," said Tara, with a more acid tongue than I'd believed her to possess, "having the three of us in your apartment is about as special an occasion as you're likely to enjoy any time soon."

Flynn interjected: "Why don't I order a pizza?"

"Oh, wonderful!" twittered Tara.

"If I'd known this was going to turn in a pajama party," I said, "I would have broken out my hairbrushes and Donny Osmond records."

"Don't be a killjoy, Miles." Peter thumbed the cork out of the champagne. It caromed off the ceiling and rebounded right into my forehead.

"Sorry," murmured Peter, while Tara suppressed a giggle.

"I suppose that's a lot like what Officer Gerald saw," I observed to myself.

"Say, why don't we invite him in?" asked Flynn. "I'll order an extra-large. With the works!"

"Do we really want our police protection to be intoxicated on the job?" I asked.

Tara was admonishing. "You bounced a golf ball off the poor guy's unmentionables. The least you could do is invite him in for a couple of drinks."

"No, the least I could do is nothing, which is what I'm going to do."

"Hello?" said Flynn into the telephone. "Is this Mario's Pizzeria? It's not? Who is this? Oh, good evening, Officer Gerald. How on earth did I reach *you*? Oh, you have a tap on this line, of course. Well, we were just about to order a pizza. And we found a bottle of champagne in Miles' icebox. What's that? You haven't eaten?"

At this point Flynn looked at me expectantly. I shook my head vigorously in a "No no no!", but Tara hissed, *"Miles!"* and I rolled my eyes and shook my head feebly in an "Okay, he can come."

Flynn said into the phone, "Would you care to join us, Officer? There'll be enough for all, I'm ordering an extra-large, with the works! You're allergic to olives? Sure, we can do that. An extra-large with the works but without olives. We'll see you in a bit, then. Take care."

He hung up and began dialing again.

This night, I could already tell, was not going to go well. I love olives.

"At least make sure it comes with green peppers," I requested of Flynn. He signaled acknowledgement.

"Hey," said Tara, lifting a notebook from my briefcase, which lay open on the kitchen counter, "what's in here?"

"Nothing," I said, hastily moving toward her for the express purpose of removing it from her hands.

"Professor of the Month Award," she read. "Everlasting House…Dr. Humphreys…Papagozzi's… poisoned…Officer Gerald…" She looked up at me. "These are notes," she said. "You're keeping notes?"

"Yes," I answered. "I'm keeping notes."

"Planning on writing a book about all of this?"

"No, I'm keeping a careful record, like a good historian. If I can connect enough of the dots, maybe I'll recognize the portrait they make and figure out what the heck is going on."

Tara set the notebook aside disinterestedly. "If it's like most connect-the-dots," she said, "it'll only be a pony, or a clown's face."

Into the silence that followed flowed Flynn's voice, on the phone with Tony's Pizzeria. "Oh, too bad," he said, guilt-ily glancing at me. "You're out of green peppers?"

I lowered my head. This night needed to go quickly and it needed never to be remembered.

"Pass," said I, "the champagne."

*   *   *

Two hours later, Peter was asleep, Tara was singing "Red River Valley," Flynn was practicing his golf swing with an imaginary club, and Officer Gerald was staring out the window.

The reason that Officer Gerald was staring out the window was that he had just concluded the story of his ill-fated relationship with a girl named Annabelle. She had broken his heart into a million pieces more than a year ago, but he was still coming to terms with the entire episode.

"She was the *most* beautiful girl," he said, his eyes fixed on a distant point.

"She treated you like dirt," I countered.

The champagne (how a solitary bottle of champagne had served to inebriate five people to this extent, I cannot account for) had loosened my tongue to an alarming degree. Ordinarily I would listen to a tale such as that of Officer Gerald and Annabelle and I would nod empathetically at strategic junctures while assiduously refraining from offering commentary and/or advice. I was, after all, a 27-year old college professor, the highlight of whose recent social life was an evening spent getting drunk while a derelict-in-his-duty policeman bent my ear about the girl who got away. What right did I have to offer commentary and/or advice? I needed someone to offer commentary and/or advice to *me*, for goodness sake.

"But I did love her so," said Gerald. He was still gazing out the window.

"She treated you like dirt," I repeated, for emphasis. "You should move on. Lots of women out there. Tons of 'em.

Single, good-looking, intelligent, the whole shmear. You're a cop, you shouldn't have trouble finding a woman."

"Not one like her," said Gerald. His gaze never faltered — out the window, into the night, like a lovesick Romeo. He was either in an advanced stage of pining or the liquor had blinded him.

If only it had deafened me.

"Not everything works out in the end," I said. My words were starting to slur. "When you think about it, every relationship is headed either for the altar or a breakup."

Gerald's gaze finally tore away from the window. He regarded me with a kind of surprised admiration. "That's one of the most profound things I've ever heard another human being say. Did you just make that up?"

"Yeah," I said off-handedly. "Look, I'm drunk, so don't take anything I say to heart, okay?"

"No, no, I'm serious," said Gerald. "That was truly profound."

"I'm *drunk*. I'm sorry, okay?"

"I'm not mad at you, I'm happy you gave me some perspective."

"Just don't put this in your report, okay?"

"I can't report this. I've had two glasses of champagne. I'm on duty!"

"Fine, fine, be that way."

"You don't know how to take a thank you, do you?"

"I said I was sorry!"

"You've had too much to drink."

Tara sang, with gusto and volume, *"Li-ving in a material world…and I am a material girl…"*

I said, "If she keeps that up we'll have the police here in no time."

Gerald brushed aside my hilarious comment as if it was a pesky gnat. A bittersweet undertone entered his voice. "I didn't start out wanting to be a policeman. I wanted to be a—"

I don't remember what else he said. It may have been truly profound. It may have been truly important. It may even have brought back his beloved Annabelle, if only he'd said it to her.

But I would never know. I had fallen asleep.

*   *   *

When I awoke and saw the figure poised over me, Tara was drunkenly dozing on the futon, while Flynn and Peter were drunkenly dozing on the floor beside me. Someone — I assumed Gerald — had draped two unzipped sleeping bags over the three of us. My first thought was that the figure *was* Officer Gerald, having just completed his task…but the shape of the figure was all wrong for Gerald, and there was a furtiveness, a menace, about the figure that didn't match Gerald's movements.

The figure spoke.

"Oh, you're awake," it said. *He* said — and not Gerald; Gerald must have returned to his post next door. But it was a man's voice. Not just a man's voice, though: a masculine voice. Deep, strong. He smelled of Old Spice and Marlboros. He wore a black mask with slits for eyes.

"Who are you?" I whispered. My head was throbbing from the champagne.

The figure crept forward. "I'm your worst nightmare."

I strained to see in the dark. "I mean, besides that."

The figure halted. "'Besides that'? Isn't that enough?"

"I mean — who are you under that mask?"

The figure crossed its arms vexedly. "If I'd wanted you to know who I was under the mask, *would I have worn the mask?*"

I craned my neck, but the figure remained indistinct. "It's...the way you move, the way you speak...I have a feeling I know you."

"You don't. Take my word for it."

"If I don't know you, why did you wear the mask?"

The figure looked at the floor and shook its head. Then the figure looked back at me. "How 'bout a police lineup, you ever think of that? How 'bout if I botch the job and you come after me for revenge, ever think of that? How 'bout if I run for office, and you recognize my face, ever think of that? You think the public is gonna elect a killer who's too stupid even to wear a mask and conceal his identity?"

"Is that why you're here? To kill me?"

"Yeah." The figure stepped toward me. "You — you don't seem too frightened."

"I'm not."

"How come?"

I shrugged noncommittally. "Could be I know something you don't."

The figure stood up straight, suddenly ready. "—There's a man behind me with a gun."

"No."

"You took the bullets out of *my* gun."

"No."

"They put out a contract on me to get rid of all the witnesses."

"No."

"You left a sealed envelope explaining everything in a safety deposit box to be opened only in the event of your death."

I said, "Would you like me to tell you what it is?"

"What haven't we covered?"

"This room is under surveillance by the police."

The figure relaxed. "Oh, you mean Gerald."

My frown turned right-side-up. "You know about Gerald?"

"Oh, sure," said the figure. "But he's asleep right now. He's had a very long day. The man's not a robot, you know. He's lucky he's not singing falsetto, after what you did to him."

Something had snapped within me that afternoon on the golf course, and it snapped again now. I jumped up off the floor, wobbled a little, caught my balance, and strode irrevocably toward the figure. "How can you people have such intimate knowledge of the details of my life and *still* not be able to kill me?"

The figure backed away.

"You *know* everything, but you can't *do* anything! You might as well be college professors!"

The figure backed over Flynn, and my television.

"I'm sick of the bunch of you! You poisoned the root beer, you poisoned the IV, you shot at me on an open golf course — *but you couldn't kill me!* You couldn't even manage to kill me when I was *drunk and asleep!*"

The figure was at the window, which it scrambled to climb out.

I pointed a gigantic finger at it and roared, "This is the most *inept* conspiracy ever!"

The figure dove from the window.

CHAPTER XIII
ZUIDER ZEE

MY DANDER WAS UP. I DON'T MEAN TO BRAG, BUT NOBODY SNEAKS into my room in the middle of the night and tries to kill me without either a) succeeding or b) hearing a mouthful from me about it. I'd given the menacing figure a mouthful, but he was merely a lackey — it was the ringleader to whom I truly wanted to give a mouthful, a mouthful he'd never forget.

I woke Flynn at six o'clock in the morning* and asked him to get dressed. Through hung over, sleep-blurred eyes he asked, "What for?"

"We're going snooping," I answered.

Neither Peter nor Tara did I stir. Peter would not have wanted to accompany us, I felt sure; and Tara would have. From Gerald, next door, we heard nothing. The champagne must have taken its toll on him, as well.

So we left them there, in pastoral slumber, and emerged out onto a rapturously splendid morning. We wore light windbreakers, dark in color, and carried flashlights, matches, and, in my front right pocket, a Swiss Army Knife given to me by my father — who never failed to remind me that he'd been given it by his father and who never failed to remind me that

---

* A sure sign that my dander *was* up, for I can count the number of times I've woken up at 6 a.m. on one finger.

he was looking forward to the day when I passed it on to my son, as if instructed to do so by Gregor Mendel himself.

We made for the woods behind my apartment building. In the dim light of dawn, sheltered in the thick blanket of low-hanging limbs and branches, it would have been difficult for anyone to watch us, or follow us. But it was just as difficult to see if anyone was watching or following us.

I had chosen the woods because they ran the length of Constant, past the College, down to Everlasting House: our destination. I had no real plan beyond this, beyond following the woods down to Everlasting House — but as mentioned, my dander was up, and I was by gosh going to take the fight to the enemy, instead of patiently waiting around to be liquidated.

I soon discovered just how impetuous this gesture was. A wall surrounded Everlasting House, a high stone wall that, on this morning, seemed to stretch vertically as the Red Sea must have seemed to the Israelites to stretch horizontally. Flynn and I gave one another a hangdog glance and set about traversing the base of the wall, hunting for a tree with overhanging limbs, or a clinging vine, or a forgotten gate with a rusty lock. After an hour and a half, however, and what must have been close to three miles of distance, it had become agonizingly apparent that this wall was not going to part, no matter how often I raised my walking stick and called down the Lord's mighty hand.

Then we heard a chugging; a low, throbbing beat. It grew louder as we crept along the wall's foundation. We broke out of the woods onto the bank of Lasting Lake — the wall continued on, rising ten feet or more above the lake's surface, all the way to its opposite bank, and into the woods on that side. Dr. Humphreys was emphatically well protected; or perhaps it was better said that Everlasting House was emphatically well protected, for I suspected that the House was a great deal more important to the "Organization" than was its occupant.

The source of the chugging was a small boat, what looked to be a converted tug, tooling along several hundred yards offshore. In faded and flaking gray paint its name was written on the prow: *Zuider Zee.*

"Look there," said Flynn, pointing. "A seam in the wall, in the middle of the lake. I'll bet it's a door."

"Yes...and I'll bet that tug makes use of it."

I jumped, and hollered, like Robinson Crusoe spying an English merchanter. Flynn joined in, waving his windbreaker. The crew of the little boat — three young men, around college age — stared at us in astonishment.

"Hey!" we yelled. "Over here! Over here!"

The men continued to stare. They seemed paralyzed — as if we had caught them engaged in illicit activity, and their only refuge lay in unblemished inaction.

I took a glimpse at Flynn, who returned my quizzical gaze.

A tall, broad man emerged from the boat's pilothouse. He wore a Greek sailor's cap and a Navy pea coat. His skin was tanned and leathery. His beard was mostly silver, partly black, and from it bloomed a corncob pipe. He moved, with a limp, through his three statuesque crewmen, then leaned his upper body well out over the side railing to gawk at us on shore.

"Ahoy!" he thundered. "What is it ye be wantin'?"

"We have a business proposition!" I shouted.

"Business, ye say? Do I look like bleedin' Adam Smith t' ye?"

"It's a chance to earn a fortune!"

"What care I for a fortune? I got me darlin' boat! I got me mates! What else do I need?"

"A new engine, from the sound of it!"

"Hang on, I'll be right over."

The boat came around in a 270-degree turn, cutting through the furrows of its own wake. Flamboyant puffs of smoke coughed out of its red-rimmed stack.

Flynn tapped me on the shoulder. "Where'd you learn to speak salty?" he asked. "You stood up to him like a regular Ensign Pulver!"

I shrugged humbly.

"Ahh..." sighed Flynn. "Look at her. Even the lowliest of ships is a comely thing!"

The *Zuider Zee* did have a shape to her, I had to admit, but "lowly" was distinctly more appropriate for it than "comely." I glanced at Flynn — he slanted over the shore with the aid of a walking stick whose tip was sunk three inches into the muddy bank. His chin jutted, and the corner of his lip twisted upward satisfactorily.

I sensed a subtle but unmistakable change in the wind. When Flynn's passions changed, the very weather itself gave notice. What was it to be this time? I wondered. Tugboats? Ships in general? The ocean? Freshwater lakes? Salty sea captains? Salty freshwater lake captains? Only time would tell.

The *Zuider Zee*'s captain's presence (and foul language, in copious amounts) was, after a time, enough to rouse his crew from their lethargy. He launched one of the three in a small pontoon that looked to have been patched so often, with squares of so many different colors, that it would have made a perfect present from Jacob to Joseph. As the pontoon drew up and bounded onto the bank, I noticed an equally reassuring

inch or so of cruddy water in its bottom, sloshing around im-
pertinently.

"Ahoy," said Flynn to the crewman, who was dressed in
a black-and-white striped shirt and blue bellbottoms.

"'Ey," said the crewman. "Name's Marky."

Flynn saluted and reached out his arm. "I'm Flynn, and
this here landlubber's Miles Hudson, Ph.D."

Yes, sir, Flynn's passion for golf, implacable and inde-
structible during its allotted time, had been suddenly and
mercilessly tossed over the side in favor of…the lore of the
sea, so far as I could tell. There was nothing to do but marvel
at the way Flynn's mind, for lack of a better word, worked, for
lack of a better word.

"'Ey, look 'ere," said Marky. His smile should have had
"Don't tread on me" written on it, it was so crooked. "Y'all's
got a fortune, right?"

"Enough to buy a boat engine, anyway," I said cagily.

Marky's eyes rolled around, leading his head, to peek
furtively back at *Zuider Zee*. Then they rolled back to settle on me. "How's about a deal?"

"A deal?"

"Aye. Gimme the money and I'll see what I can do."

Over the past couple of days I had been forced to put up
with more than my fair share of idiots. I was slowly learning
how to handle them. I decided to speak unambiguously.

"You will take us to your captain and you will not open
your mouth again in our presence, because if you do I will no-
tify your captain that you are a mutineer. Is that clear?"

Marky froze, then nodded quickly. He gestured for us to
enter the pontoon.

"Forget Pulver," said Flynn, chuckling. "You're a regular Captain Nemo!"

Marky pushed the bow around to face the *Zuider Zee*, jumped in, and powered up the motor. We shot across the lake, bouncing over undulations in the lake surface that, to my landlubbing eyes, appeared rather large. I turned to make mention of this to Flynn, but quickly thought better of it. He'd only have made some comment along the lines of "Hoist the maintopgallantmizzenstayshrouds, Cap'n!"

Marky brought the pontoon in on the tug's port side. We climbed a rope ladder and hopped onto the *Zuider Zee*'s deck. The captain was not quite as imposing up-close, standing as he did six inches shorter than either Flynn or me.

"Permission to come aboard?" asked Flynn.

"Granted," rumbled the captain. "Now what is it ye be wantin' in return for a brand spankin' new motor engine?" He had an accent, too, noticeable when he wasn't blaring: generic Old World. Given the name of his boat, I took him to be Dutch.

"We want safe passage through that wall, onto the grounds of Everlasting House," I informed him.

The captain's eyes narrowed like a cat's when the light is turned on. "Everlastin' House..." He stepped very close to me, his corncob pipe brushing my cheek. His breath smelled of tobacco and Doublemint gum. "What ye be wantin' at Everlastin' House?"

I stood my ground, not taking my eyes from his. "Not your concern. Take us in, drop us off, wait for us, bring us back out. That's all you have to do. For that, you get a brand spankin' new motor engine."

He chomped on his pipe stem, rotating the corncob in circles that pelted my nose. "That's all we gotta do? In, wait, out?"

"That's all," I said.

"Deal," he said, punching a chunky hand toward me.

I shook it. "Deal."

He backed away, starting for the pilothouse. "Should be no troubles. We're contracted to Mr. Humphreys to get all the golf balls out o' the lake what he hits int' it. Marky there dolls himself up in SCUBA gear." The captain swept past Marky and the two other crewmen and disappeared into the pilothouse. The crewmen kept their distance, surveilling me worriedly. "Gen'ly," came the captain's voice, "we do it in the middle o' the week, but shouldn't seem too amiss if we're a bit early. When do I get my motor?"

"Soon as we're out, Captain...?"

His head popped out of a window in the pilothouse. "Queeg," he said. "Cap'n A.B. Queeg." His head popped back in.

"Queeg? Your name is Queeg?"

His head popped back out. "Aye. So?"

"Oh, nothing," I said, but didn't mean it.

"What do the A and the B stand for?" asked Flynn.

The captain popped his head back in. "Trust me, ye'll not be wantin' t' know."

"Why not?" protested Flynn. "I think if we're hiring your boat and crew, we have a right to know your full name."

I applied a delicate pressure to Flynn's elbow, the message behind which was, "Stop with the talking already." I called jovially to the captain, "Just so long as the A doesn't stand for Ahab and the B for Bligh!"

His head popped out the window again. He wore an uncomfortable expression. "Er, no," he said, his left eye starting to twitch. "Whatever the A and the B stand for, it sure as shootin' ain't Ahab Bligh. I mean to say, Ahab Bligh Queeg? Who'd name their child *that*? Only a pitiless and heartless stepmother, that's who! When a mother dies in childbirth and a father's taken advantage of by a schemin' witch who swoops in and takes the baby as her own and has the temerity to insist on providin' the child's name, *that's* how you get a boy called Ahab Bligh Queeg!"

The captain wiped the spittle from his lips, his chest heaving with emotion.

Flynn said, "What's so bad about Ahab Bligh Queeg? Sounds like a fine old seafarin' name to me!"

The captain snarled "Bah!" and ducked his head back into the pilothouse before the topic could be explored further.

Flynn shrugged his shoulders. He inhaled, breathing deep the watery air. He mused, almost to himself, "Wasn't there a Captain Ahab in a movie or something?"

It occurred to me that my expertise at dealing with idiots might not be such a recent development after all.

CHAPTER XIV
QUEEG

CAPTAIN'S QUEEG'S* CREW SNAPPED TO ATTENTION FOR HIS ORDERS, and carried them out without question. He steered the boat well, from what little I know of boat-steering — i.e., the boat went where it was supposed to. The mechanism for the sea-door in the wall, Queeg enlightened us, was inside Everlasting House. He would need to radio and petition "that stuffy limey" (Jenkins?) to open it — unfortunately, the radio was in the boathouse at the dock, on the other side of the lake.

"You don't have a radio on board?" I asked.

"Nope," said Queeg. "If y'ever want to come back for a second ride, I'll trade ye for a ship-to-shore jobbie."

"We won't be needing a second ride," I said, devoutly hoping this would turn out to be true.

"Suit yerself," said the captain, returning to absentmind-edly humming "Born Free."

I went out on deck, where Flynn was watching Marky and the two other crewmen, names of Willie (green-and-white

---

* The man's name really was Queeg — it was there on his tugboat opera-tor's license, taped above the window in the pilothouse: "A.B. Queeg." I was baffled, because if your name was Ahab Bligh Queeg and your occu-pation remotely pertained to the sea, would you not change either your name or your occupation? To be honest, if my name was Ahab Bligh Queeg, I'd change it no matter what my occupation pertained to.

striped) and Greenie (red-and-white striped), practice their seamanship. Or lakemanship, as the case may be.

"Aren't they wonderful?" said Flynn. "Full of vim and vigor! Fresh air in their lungs, facing life with a simple purpose few of us can fathom...what was it like, Miles, aboard a three-masted schooner off the Guinea coast?"

I had long since realized that Flynn would always be, in some essential way, unfathomable to me. When his passion for a topic welled, he began right away to remember facts and figures about the topic as if by genetic memory; and after his passion had crested and ebbed, those facts and figures slipped from their moorings and drifted into the night, gone forever, as new facts and figures about his new passion effortlessly slid into the empty spaces left behind. In this fashion Flynn could at one moment not for the life of him recall where he'd heard of Captain Ahab and in the next be speaking with authority of three-masted schooners off the Guinea coast. There was nothing to do but marvel, etc.

I felt moisture on my forearm. I wiped it off with my fingers, but felt more moistures — drops of rain, increasing in speed and volume.

"A squall!" exclaimed Flynn with delight. "Perfect!"

The lake, I could not help but observe, was rapidly turning tempestuous. What had been a clear-blue sky had become battleship gray in less than five minutes.

Spray from a breaker washed over the deck and showered Flynn and I. He hooted. I sputtered. The rain now fell in sheets, as if it had been collated; thin, plentiful, painful sheets.

"*Lookee!*" cried Willie.

He was pointing at the nor'eastern sky. Black, black, black, it was — as if the daylight had spread like a curtain to let the starless night rush in. The edge of it was spreading fast, a bottle of spilt ink, threatening to swallow us.

"Get inside!" bellowed Queeg, who'd come out on deck to witness the weather for himself. "Batten the hatches!"

Marky, Willie, and Greenie dove down through three separate deck hatches, then pulled them shut and twisted them tight.

I looked at Flynn.

"Do we have to go inside?" he asked, with all seriousness. "Can't we ride out the storm out here?"

I grabbed his shoulder and pulled him through the plummeting rains and the driving winds, across the slickened deck into the pilothouse. Even inside, the storm's volume was clamorous. I yelled above the fury, "I don't think we can ride it out in here, much less out there!"

"Get below!" ordered Queeg. "No room for amateurs up here!"

Flynn gave him a wounded expression. I grabbed Flynn's shoulder once again and hustled him down the steep stairwell into the lounge. Marky, Willie, and Greenie gaped at us. "'Ey," said Willie and Greenie. Marky said nothing. He may have inclined his head in a feeble greeting.

Our clothes were soaked, our bones were chilled — the rocking and swaying and jumping of the boat, though, made holding a cup of coffee or cocoa an impossible proposition, as my thrice-blistered fingers attested. In desperation I grabbed a heavy blanket from a locker, wrapped it tautly about myself, and anchored myself firmly in a not-too-uncomfortable chair, settling in for a nice, pleasant bout of seasickness.

Flynn paced anxiously, glancing often at the stairwell. I myself was torn, for on the one hand, this was a formidable storm, and Queeg might be requiring assistance and regretting his decision to banish us from the upper deck; on the other hand, we truly were, Flynn's opinions notwithstanding, amateurs — and if Marky, Willie, and Greenie weren't up there helping their captain and weren't feeling torn about it, why should I be?

Speaking of whom, they stared at us in the same way the exhibits stare at the visitors in a museum. It was aggravating, but I was too tired and too cold and too wet to go to all the trouble of saying, "Please stop." Instead I closed my eyes, so I wouldn't have to look at them looking at me.

Not much time passed before Greenie said, out of the blue, "Cap'n respects you. Plain as day, he does."

I said, without opening my eyes, "A new engine'll do that to a man."

"Nah, it's more than that. He *likes* you. You're his kind o' people."

This frightened me immeasurably. I opened my eyes.

Greenie looked at the floor. "Cap'n's quite mad, you know."

I stopped the laugh just at the top of my throat. "Is he?"

"Aye. That's plain as day, too. We three've had to live with it, day in, day out, fer year after year after year after year."

"Why don't you quit? Find other work."

Greenie looked at me as if I was missing the most obvious of all of God's truths. "We *can't* quit, ya daffy. We're his sons."

I closed my eyes and, despite enormous odds, tried to go to sleep.

"Endless weeks, months, *years* o' wearin' these unsightly pullovers," Greenie continued bitterly. "Horizontal stripes? Of this width? At our age? He won't let us quit, ya see. Well — maybe he would, but none of us has the guts to ask him. 'Cause we know he's mad, ya see. Why d'ya think it's takin' so long just to get back to the dock? Thirty minutes to go thirty yards? Is that reasonable? We could have got there in the pontoon a half hour ago!"

"Why are you telling me this?" I asked tiredly. "To comfort me?"

"We want ya to relieve him," said Greenie, shaking his head vigorously in the affirmative, as did his brothers.

"*Relieve* him?"

"Aye! Take command o' this vessel."

"I wouldn't have the first idea how to—"

"Mister, mister. *We'll* work the thing — you just have to take control of it."

If Queeg were mad, madness was hereditary. "This," I said, "is a tiny boat in a tiny lake in a tiny town in central California. What happens here is *sincerely* not that important to anyone but yourselves. If you want to free yourselves from the bondage you imagine yourselves to be in, you'll have to do it on your own!"

Greenie had evidently heard everything I'd said except the part where I'd been talking. He extended a brotherly forearm. "Will you join in our crusade?"

"Who will be strong, and stand with me?" said Willie.

Marky rose to his feet in triumph. "Somewhere beyond the *Zuider Zee* is there a world you long to see?"

But he fell right back down into his seat as the door to the pilothouse at the top of the stairwell clattered open.

Queeg's black boots descended. He came down into the lounge and, pouring himself a cup of coffee, looked at each of us in turn.

"We're here," he said.

"You've already radioed Everlasting House?"

"Not 'here' the dock, 'here' the House."

Momentarily engaging the three senses I had not been making use of, I realized that the boat had stopped its jerky motion. In fact the boat had stopped *all* motion — the engine wasn't running.

"We're at Everlasting House?" I asked dubiously.

"Not on her front door, but close enough," said Queeg, sipping his coffee. He reached into his pocket and pulled something out, but kept his fingers clenched tightly around whatever it was. "Storm's over. Rough goin' for a spot, but made it through hunky-dory."

For an instant none of my senses would engage. Queeg had piloted us to the dock, tied up, gone inside and radioed Everlasting House, piloted us through the sea-gate and landed us safely at our objective...all in a gale that would have set records in the North Atlantic.

Flynn danced up the stairs, and twirled at the top, a là Julie Andrews. He did not begin to sing, but he was about to, and I saw the need to remove him a large distance from the lake, in a hurry.

"Thanks for all your help, Captain," I said. I reached to shake his right hand. For him to shake mine, he had to switch the objects he had pulled from his pocket to his left hand. I caught a fleeting glimpse of those objects and sucked in my breath — luckily it takes a few seconds for one's hand to go clammy, and all Queeg felt was a warm, firm handshake.

"Let's go on deck," said Queeg, pushing me before him. I climbed the stairs — Flynn had mounted the crow's nest and was belting out "Spanish Ladies" — with Queeg right behind me. He slammed shut the door to the lounge.

"They gave ye the 'Mad Dog Queeg' routine, di'nt they?"

My smile was wan. "Yes, they did." I added, "I don't believe it," but my delivery was not especially credible.

He glanced down at his left hand, and spread his fingers, and snapped the two steel balls together. He grinned at me. "Medically speakin', no, I'm not mad. But ye can't live your every day sailin' about a small lake with yer three grown sons aboard and be wholly normal."

He shook his head. "'Tis a puzzlement…their mother went to the Sorbonnes fer a year, I'm a graduate o' the Academy — how'd our couplin' result in three boys each of which is thicker than the last? Put 'em all together and they couldn't outwit Elmer Fudd."

The steel balls rattled noisily in his palm. "My doctor recommended these. Therapeutic, he said."

The balls crescendoed and fell silent. "Ye'd better go, do what ye came to do," said Queeg. "We'll be here when ye're done."

"Thanks again," I said, and began the climb to the crow's nest to collect Flynn.

Below me, Queeg yanked open the door to the lounge and stormed down the stairs. "What d'ye think ye're doin', ye mindless jellies? Talkin' 'bout yer ol' man behind his back!"

There followed a series of plunks that sounded suspiciously like steel balls rebounding off next-generation Dutch foreheads.

CHAPTER XV
THE LIBRARY

WE HAD CIRCUMVENTED EVERLASTING HOUSE'S SURROUNDING wall, but we still needed to gain entrance to the House proper. The day was moving toward midmorning, a time when I would have anticipated the grounds to be alive with gardeners, beekeepers, tree pruners, and the like — but from the banks of Lasting Lake to the very walls of Everlasting House itself we spied not a single person. The morning's torrent had left the carefully-cultivated lawns moist and slippery, making them dangerous and noisy to walk on; but in the absence of ears to hear our commotion, we soon decided vigilance was unnecessary and tramped across the glossy fields as quickly as we could.

Our advance on Everlasting House was from the south. The golf course, skirting as it did the lake, was visible to the west, as were the polo grounds to the east. The rear of the house — like the dark side of the moon — was a side no one had seen, or at least that no one had reported seeing, but its appearance was equal to its opposite number's. Roderick Blanding had completed Patrick Hester's San Simeon, his glittering, shimmering, gleaming San Simeon, brilliant in the post-deluge sunshine.

Flynn's head tilted backward as his eyes tracked up the House's three stories, each of which presented a convincing façade of utterly impenetrability. "This'll be challenging," he said. "But if I can infiltrate the Hermitage*, I can infiltrate *this*."

I said, without conviction, "We could get lucky and they'll have left a window or a door unlocked."

Flynn's head rotated forty-five degrees and alighted on me. His normally festive aspect was replaced by one of "Sure, Miles."

We proceeded to check the ground-floor windows, careful not to touch them, only to examine their sliding locks. We had disqualified all of the rear windows and were working on the east side when, out of the corner of my eye, I saw Flynn's feet fly backwards from under him — he twirled a complete spin in the air and came down squarely on the soles of his feet. The entire incident so surprised him that he sank to the mossy ground, dazed and disoriented.

"Be careful!" I implored, racing to his side. "This grass is slick!"

"It wasn't the grass!" he retorted. "I tripped on something!"

He ran his hands through the matted grass around him and promptly discovered a metal handle, which, after further investigation, proved to belong to a metal door that had been buried by a layer of moss and was seemingly long forgotten by the residents of Everlasting House. A rusted chain looped through the handle, but the lock on the chain was unfastened. Flynn removed it and pulled open the door.

We were confronted by a darkness that made the earlier storm clouds appear friendly. Flynn brought out his flashlight and shone its beam down into the pitch. A circular stairwell wound into the shadows like a helix of DNA. The steps were terrifyingly narrow.

---

* Which he had (or claimed to have), during a War of 1812 phase.

Flynn smiled at me like a schoolboy who'd found a secret stash of fireworks. "We go in?"

Ordinarily my first instinct would have been to fake a cough to give myself time to construct a fitting response, something that would not sound cowardly and yet would have resulted in my *not* having to descend those stairs, but as I have mentioned, my dander was up — I was not about to be put off by a darkness so black it had an event horizon.

Flynn's voice echoed back from the depths: *We go in?*

The echo meant the steps had an end; but the echo had taken its time, which meant the end was a long way down.

I swallowed the cough. "Sure," I said. "Er...right behind you."

*   *   *

Flynn crawled slowly ahead of me, making certain of the next foothold before removing his weight from the last. I trod carefully behind him, and at a snail's pace, for even at a crawl, the endless tight rotation of the downward spiral was making me light-headed and dizzy. My legs, also, were beginning to ache; I regretted having skipped so many visits to the gym. I warned Flynn that we'd better reach the foot of the stairs before too much longer, or we'd reach them before too much longer in any event when I misstepped and took both of us to the bottom in a crumpled heap.

"Never fear!" replied Flynn. "Remember my time with the Clowns!"

This was a reference to Constant's professional softball team, for whom Flynn had served as mascot for three weeks the previous summer. He had dedicated himself wholly to the task, losing ten pounds and getting into the best shape of his life just in time for that phase to end and his Canadian Mountie phase to begin. Since that time he'd regained the weight and put on more, but he still considered himself to be in tremendous shape, and quite capable of putting a halt to any tumble I might care to take. I was not so confident, and prayed we'd reach the bottom soon.

Reach it we did — at, by my watch, 11:38 a.m. A narrow corridor led to a broader entryway housing a steel hatch. I walked ahead and put my ear to it, but heard nothing beyond. I indicated as such to Flynn. He held out his arm by way of granting permission for me to continue. I turned the latch and pushed the hatch open.

A flickering light seeped in around the edges of the hatch, flooding our entryway as the opening widened. The first thing to catch my eye was that the room ahead was lit by torches spaced high along the walls, perched in ornate sconces. The second thing to catch my eye were shelves, shelves crowded with volume after volume — not little romance paperbacks, either, but oversized leather-bound editions, bursting from the shelves like a poorly-packed parachute.

The room was circular and, so far as I could see, boasted no entrance other than the one we stood in — but the other side of the steel door, I had noticed while venturing into the chamber, was camouflaged so as to appear flush with the rocky wall around it. When closed it would be all but invisible. If there were there other doors to this archive, I reasoned, they might be hidden via the same drab disguise.

At the center of the room's circle sat a large globe, and beside it a cushioned chair, in the seat of which laid a black-bound tome. I tiptoed forward. That part of the globe turned to face the chair was, roughly speaking, the Americas. A red circle had been marked over central California — right over Constant College — and the same sort of brand had been applied to a number of cities spread across the planet: Sydney; Cairo; Hong Kong; Johannesburg; Sao Paulo; George Town,

Grand Cayman; and in Europe, Geneva, Paris, Istanbul, Stockholm, Munich, Rome, and London; and in the United States, aside from Constant, also New York, Los Angeles, Chicago, Denver, Houston, and Atlanta.

"Flynn," I said — he was perusing an especially overcrowded section, probably wishing he'd known of this place during his antiques phase — "don't touch anything. If we disturb the dust, they'll know someone's been snooping."

"From the depth of the dust in here, old sod, no one's been here for decades — if not centuries. Who's going to know? Besides, these are *books*. We won't find out anything if we don't open them."

"All right — but put them back exactly as you found them."

He beamed and returned to the shelves.

I, meanwhile, was intrigued by the tome on the chair — for it, unlike every other tome in this library, had no layer of dust on its cover at all. A bookmark had been placed about halfway through its pages, so I opened to that page. In an archaic hand was a diary entry, dated July 1, 1926.

> *The formula is nearly complete. Barbara has invited certain of the family to the house for the ceremonial reading of the Preamble and the Declaration on the 4th. Never mind that this so-called ceremony has not occurred before, nor ever will again. Roderick is no fool, and neither is William — they will see through Barbara's deceptions easily enough. I have told her again and again that we cannot maintain absolute secrecy in perpetuity. We must either include the family or remove ourselves from them.*

Nowhere in the front-pages did the diarist name himself, but he didn't need to — the diary was that of Patrick Hester. The date would place Patrick's age at 45. His sister, Barbara Blanding, would have been 23. Patrick had written that Barbara's "deceptions" would be seen through easily, but what deception was she engaged in? Her addiction to opium? Was the "ceremony" to which he referred some sort of opium-fueled ritual?

In any case, it was clear enough that Barbara was guilty of secrecy, if not outright villainy — but then I had to remind myself that this was Patrick's diary, reflecting Patrick's point of view, and what Patrick considered to be villainy in the summer of 1926 might, more than three-quarters of a century later, be considered a minor traffic violation.

I flipped through the diary's pages. The dates ran from early 1925 to February 14, 1929: the day Patrick Hester had died. Strange, that the man's life should end on the same day he ran out of pages in his diary. The final entry read:

> *Barbara cannot be reasoned with. Every day we argue more. It was my decision to proceed, but the project must not now be aborted, however discouraging its preliminary results. If she has her way then all that we have done will be for naught. We are brother and sister, yet she no longer trusts me and I no longer trust her. I fear what she might do if backed into a corner. I have spoken to Roderick, as a precaution.*

I closed the book and gazed at its cover. The entries verified that, at the least, tensions existed between Patrick and his sister. But tensions were not sufficient evidence, 81 years after the fact, to convict Barbara Blanding of murder. Even her opium addiction was merely a rumor, not a matter of fact.

The larger question, however, was: How had Patrick Hester's diary come to be in a hidden library under Everlasting House? Patrick had spent much of his time in Constant during the house's construction, but he'd been in Atlanta at the time of his death, and judging by the final entry, he'd had the diary in his possession right up until the end. Had Roderick found the diary after Patrick's death and brought it with him to Constant? Had Roderick known of Barbara's villainy? Was Barbara a villain to begin with? What was the "project" in which she and Patrick were engaged?

Whatever the truth, the historian in me found all of this fascinating. Source material on the history of Everlasting House was difficult to come by — those few dedicated souls who had taken up the task of chronicling the House's past had found precious little beyond the widely-accepted folklore related earlier. No one now alive could say for sure just where that folklore had originated, but through the years it had cemented into accepted fact.

Historian's antennae thus aquiver, I debated whether to take the diary with me. Despite Flynn's protestations, *somebody* had been reading it, and recently — but I couldn't leave it behind, not if I wanted to go on calling myself a history professor. The whole strange, sordid history of the Hesters and the Blandings might be between the covers of the book I held in my hands!

"Miles," interrupted Flynn in a somber tone, "come here."

I knew the news could not be good, if Flynn wasn't referring to me with a noun preceded by "old." He had lain open in his arms a tall, fat tome with **Birthings** stamped in a powdery blue on its cover. He struggled to hold the book open, it was so large, and as it nearly slipped from his hands, four pages fell out, swirling to the floor in a feather-like dance.

I gave Flynn a curious frown. He replied with a gesture that strongly implied I could be using the time I was using to frown at him to, oh, I don't know, pick up the pages?

I reached down and retrieved them. They were printed on parchment and bore official seals, laminated in gold ink: birth certificates.

Robert Toones, 1926.   Mitchell Hand, 1941.   Patricia Yardley, 1919. Each born in Colorado Springs, Colorado.

Flynn stared at me gravely. I looked at the next birth certificate.

Tara Fury, Atlanta, 1980.

I drew a breath, finding it surprisingly easy. "Wow," I think I said.

"That's not all," said Flynn. He bent the book, and let its pages turn of themselves. The way things had been going, I should have known what Flynn was about to show me, but it came as a complete surprise.

The birth certificate affixed to the page was gray, faded with age. Along the top ran the words "County of Shawnee, Kansas." Along the middle ran the name *Miles Hudson*.

CHAPTER XVI
IN THE BLACK

I WAS NUMBED — CHILLED TO THE BONE — FROZEN WHERE I STOOD. What in the name of Benjamin Spock was my birth certificate — not a Xerox, not a fax, but the original, torn from the Shawnee County Ledger — doing buried in a forgotten basement of Everlasting House?

The diary — the business with Patrick and Barbara and Roderick — may or may not have had any bearing on the "organization," Dr. Humphreys, the attempts on my and Tara's life, etc.; here, though, was a development linking me — undeniably, irrevocably linking me — to Everlasting House. My birth certificate was in a book full of birth certificates in a mysterious library located beneath a legendary house whose owner belonged to an organization that wanted me dead, or at least out of the way. Try saying that ten times fast, and then ask yourself, as I did, *Why* was my birth certificate in a book full of birth certificates in a mysterious library located beneath a legendary house whose owner belonged to an organization that wanted me dead, or at least out of the way?

This development, like so many other developments recently, raised an exponential number of questions and answered exactly zero. So many questions shot into my mind, in fact, that I couldn't settle on any one of them — if the trek down the stairs had threatened to dizzify my brain, this new development completed the job. I couldn't think straight. I couldn't even think crooked. I needed to sit down.

"Shhh!" hissed Flynn. "Do you hear that?"

"Hear what?"

"Shhh!" Flynn held his finger up to his lips.

I whispered, as softly as I could, "I don't hear anything."

He shook his head, again shushing me, his face intent with concentration.

"It sounds like...*chanting*..."

I strained to hear, holding myself entirely motionless. At first I heard nothing, but then, faint as a hypnotist's suggestion, distant as a desert oasis, I heard it. It gained in strength, becoming easier to distinguish, as we stood there, posed ridiculously with our hands cupped to our ears: a steady, pounding rhythm, ominous and sinister.

"What *is* that?" asked Flynn.

"It ain't the 4-H Club," I rejoindered wittily.

We circumnavigated the room, pausing every few feet to listen, attempting to pinpoint the direction from which the sound originated. But the library's acoustic properties were such that wherever we moved, the sound remained the same...as if the library was a kind of reverse whispering room.

A flash of inspiration returned to my mind the hatch through which we'd entered, and how it had been concealed on this side. If that hatch had a mechanism by which it could be opened from inside the room, that mechanism must be concealed — and, having seen more than a few late-night horror films, I thought I knew where.

I pulled the chair toward the wall and stepped up onto it. My fingers just reached the underside of a torch's sconce. Rising up on my toes, I brushed my fingers along its base, hoping to turn the sconce...but the sconce was already loose, and spun right out of its socket. The torch fell to the floor, singeing my sleeve along the way.

Flynn quickly stamped out the flame. In doing so he applied just the right touch of pressure to a plate in the floor. Two of the giant bookshelves rotated on their axes, slapping me right off the chair and nearly crushing Flynn.

He was, unsurprisingly, undaunted. Lying on his backside, grinning ear to ear, he chirped, "Found it!"

Before us lay another dark passageway. The chanting, now that the shelves were no longer acting as dampeners, was extremely close and extremely loud. Flynn and I skulked into the passage, following the sound. We dared not turn on the flashlight, but we didn't need it, as the corner ahead of us was starkly illuminated by an unseen light beyond. We approached the corner, stuck our heads around it, and were — though this was becoming for me as routine as blinking — flabbergasted.

We stood on a small ledge, below which a natural cavern the size of New Zealand spread out, a cavern whose floor was covered in every direction with figures in black robes with black hoods. None of them were facing us, but rather faced the opposite direction, toward a stage that had been carved from, I would guess, obsidian — it gleamed like my dad's shoes used to on Sunday morning. The chanting of this gathered host was resounding, not only because every one of them was putting their heart and soul into out-screaming their brethren (and sistren), but also because the echo, relentlessly seeking an exit, reverberated about the cavern like a pinball. Before, the chant had been too soft to decipher; now, it was too loud.

One of the black-robed figures stepped up onto the stage. The chant disintegrated into a resounding ovation. The black robe put out his arms, motioning for silence. He began to speak. He wore a cordless microphone, apparently, for we heard his words quite plainly.

"My friends — the final stage has arrived. Our spirit must not lag! Our devotion must not be found wanting! The culmination of our long struggle is upon us — *we must not falter!"*

The black-robed audience exploded in applause. Something in the speaker's voice was familiar to me...the near-hysteria, the trill of emotion...but I couldn't place it.

"My friends," he went on, "you will witness the climax of eight decades of planning! You will witness the birth of a brave new world! Comprehend, if you can, your place in history! *You* are the chosen ones! *The chosen leaders of the brave new world!"*

The audience exploded again. I had to put my hands over my ears — a mistake, for I had unconsciously been leaning over the edge, supporting myself with my forearms. My upper body toppled over and, despite Flynn's valiant attempts to grab hold of me, my lower body was not far behind. I turned in the air, much as Flynn had done in discovering the storm doors, and flopped to the ground, ten feet below, not flat on my feet, but flat on my back.

I could not move for an interval, during which I stared up at Flynn, who waved his arms wildly and silently mouthed a variety of phrases that I failed to interpret. I was worried that he would draw attention to himself with his gesticulations, or that I had drawn attention to myself with my pratfall, but in that cacophonous chamber, we could have exchanged gunfire and none of the black robes would have noticed.

When at last my spine stopped its spasming, I rolled over and lifted myself tenderly to my knees. By fortuitous chance, I had fallen behind the mass of black robes. By unfortuitous chance, I was stuck in an alcove behind hundreds of maniacal individuals in black robes.

I pressed against the stone wall, the shadows hiding parts of me, at least, and shuffled forward. I had missed a good chunk of the speaker's speech whilst incoherent on my back, but I was fairly sure that I'd grasped its essential gist — Us Good, Them Bad* — so my objective was simply to get out of there, posthaste. I was brought to a full stop, however, by the fleeting sight of the profile inside one of the black hoods. I came out of the shadows, so dazed from what I'd seen that safety unobtrusively slipped to the back seat of my mental bus. I took a moment to scrutinize the profiles of other black robes in the rear of the crowd, though "scrutinize" is here used in the sense of "gawk at without regard to consequence."

I knew these people. These people who were dressed up in black robes with black hoods and had come to this secret cavern beneath Everlasting House to chant unintelligibly and applaud an apocalyptic speech given by a guy also in a black robe who had, I must say, quite an excellent public speaking voice.

I knew these people. Some I knew personally, some I had seen only in yearbook photographs.

Each and every one of them had at some point in their careers won the Professor Of The Month Award.

---

* This is the essential gist of 90% of all speeches ever given.

CHAPTER XVII
LE MONDE

THE FOG ENSHROUDING MY BRAIN DISSIPATED SLIGHTLY, FROM A thick pea soup to a grainy cream of vegetable. I had joked with Peter that the Professor Of The Month Award was not bestowed for professorial proficiency, and as it turned out I'd been accidentally right — it wasn't bestowed for professorial proficiency, it was bestowed as a token of acceptance into, or membership in good standing of, this black-robed group, which viewed itself as the harbinger of a "brave new world."

Here was the organized organization in which Dr. Humphreys was a minor pawn, the organization which had attempted to kill Tara once, and me more than once. Why they'd attempted to kill me was a question now cast in a different light — was it possible they wanted me dead because they'd given me the Award by mistake? Or because I hadn't responded to receiving the Award the way they'd expected me—

Of course! Dr. Humphreys and his mixed-up handshakes! I was supposed to accept the Award with *a specific handshake!* A *code!* An acknowledgment of the true meaning of the Award!

And I, all unknowing, had flatly refused to answer that code as I should have. No wonder Dr. Humphreys had tried eighteen different ways to get me to shake his hand! Whatever combinations of left hand/right hand I'd tried, obviously none of them had been the *right* one.

So that's what this was all about? They wanted me dead because I hadn't properly returned Dr. Humphreys' hand-shake?

A silly excuse to kill a man, but if there's one thing a cave full of college faculty in black robes will show you, it's that things have gotten silly.

I turned my attention back to my immediate surroundings. I realized, thinking my tactics through a second time, that slithering along the wall was not the wisest course of action — I was needlessly risking discovery. These people didn't live down here. Sooner or later they would leave, and then my withdrawal could be nice and quiet and safely unobserved. Nonchalantly, I back-walked toward the alcove.

The speaker still had not finished his monologue. He seemed to be saying the same thing over and over again, but with different words. Periodically the audience would again applaud furiously, and he would nod and preen a bit. *No way he's a professor, too,* I thought. *No one's nodding off during* this *lecture.*

As he resumed his oratorizing, I looked down just in time to avoid tripping over an ankle-high rock on the floor of the cavern. I let out a silent "Whew" and—

A cold, hard hand locked itself over my mouth. An irresistible force pulled me backwards, and spun me around into the alcove. My back smashed against the wall, a grunt of pain escaping my lips. Little flashes of light were all I could see, but through them I gradually made out my attacker.

He wore a black robe, oddly enough, and confronted me with hands rolled into fists. The body beneath the robe gave an appearance of solid, sturdy confidence — the sort of person who could kill me in twelve assorted ways before my brain even recorded that his hands had moved. I could think of nothing to do other than put up my hands in the universal gesture of "Please inform my parents of the whereabouts of my body."

The tension in his body slackened, and he removed the hood from his head, unveiling features that were…well, how can I describe him? He was, objectively and heterosexually speaking, the most handsome man I have ever seen. Dark hair, perfectly tanned skin, piercing blue eyes, a jaw line that could have cut crystal — he was the embodiment of every woman's fantasy, and quite a few men's, too. I felt not just inadequate, but dirty, *unclean*, by comparison. Who was I to call myself a man while such as he roamed the earth?

He smiled, and I felt my teeth must look like a bowl of corn niblets, next to his.

"Steady, Miles," he said, in a voice at once soft and definite. "I'm a friend."

That voice — *the caller! The elusive caller!*

"Why weren't you at Papagozzi's?" I said, in a voice at once soft and shaky.

"Too hazardous, Miles. Their people were all over that restaurant."

I glowered at him for a considerable while. "Friends" don't let friends knowingly walk into a dangerous situation where they might conceivably be, to pick a random example, *poisoned*, now, do they?

When I felt I'd silently recriminated him enough, I asked, "Who are you?"

He glowed with reassurance. "Le Monde. Jacques Le Monde."

"You're French?"

"Yes."

"You don't have an accent. You could be from Iowa."

My voice had risen in volume, as voices will, impudently seeking their own level, and at this last outburst one of the black robes nearest us turned his head to the left. What kept him from turning right around and seeing me engaged in conversation with one of his fellow conspirators, I can only credit to my guardian angel.[*]

Le Monde smiled benignly. "It would be better if you were to let me do the talking, Miles. I am expert at what I do — be it skiing the Austrian Alps in a blizzard with a broken leg while recovering from dysentery or speaking American English with no trace of my mother tongue with such phenomenal precision of frequency and amplitude that only your ears can hear me."

I nodded, because he was so handsome that it was impossible to believe he might be exaggerating.

"I am with the Sûreté, Miles. —You have heard of us?"

I nodded again. The Sûreté is the French police force.

"We have been investigating this UNKNOWN conspiracy for many years. They are on the verge of something big, very big. Happily, I am on the verge of blowing the entire operation sky-high. *Very* sky-high."

He saw the question in my eyes.

"Yes, Miles, there is more, much more, to this than college professors in black robes. Trust me — regarding this conspiracy, you are a child. An innocent. *C'est adorable*, in its way." He smiled. But the smile did not last long. "They are everywhere, Miles. In every country, every government, every city. They are worldwide."

He saw another question in my eyes.

---

[*] Who was either working overtime or had gone out on strike, I couldn't figure out which.

"You are wondering how this is possible, how they can do it without being discovered. The Sûreté knows all too well that the difficulty lies not in uncovering the conspiracy — the difficulty lies in living long enough to share what you have learned. There have been three other agents of the Sûreté on this case. I honor their memories, but — they were not *me*."

He saw the third question in my eyes. The man was uncanny.

"Why did I telephone you? Because your reaction to receiving the Professor Of The Month Award was wrong. *Too* wrong. They give this Award to Constant College initiates for duty above and beyond the call. Would it surprise you to hear that this college is the training ground for most of their agents on the West Coast?"

No, after everything I'd witnessed, nothing surprised me anymore, including his seeing the fourth question in my eyes.

"But you are not an initiate, not an agent — why should they give *you* the Award? Ah, Miles, talking to you reminds me of how ignorant I was when I began this investigation, twelve years ago—"

"Twelve *years?*" I sputtered.

His look was understanding, but it also conveyed, politely, the unambiguous message that two words out of my mouth were two words too many.

"You see how large this is," he continued. "How widespread. Even I — Jacques Le Monde! — am using up a lifetime dismantling it. I shall elaborate. In the contiguous forty-eight United States, this conspiracy has been divided for decades, cut in twain: an Eastern Wing and a Western Wing. The split occurred, for reasons I have not been able to determine, just prior to the Second World War. Roderick Blanding took in a faction of dissidents led by a man named Davis Cranston — the Cranstons were related to the Blandings by marriage.

Davis created and organized the Western Wing and served as its leader for many years, just as his twin brother Theodore led the Eastern Wing.

"Davis died in 1971, and the Western Wing has had four leaders since then, the latest being a brilliantly diabolical young man named Luther Ado. (He's capital at chemin de fer — the devil played me to a draw, and *nobody* does that, I assure you.) That's him addressing the troops now. The two wings were never truly belligerent — they were simply competitive. They are, ultimately, pursuing the same goals. Probably it is a good thing for the world that they have *not* been acting in concert, for they would already have achieved many more of those goals than they have.

"Recently there has been talk of re-merging the two wings, back into the dominant force they were before they split. Seven months ago, the Eastern Wing was rumored to have sent an emissary to Constant, a member of their inner circle, to negotiate with the Western Wing. But contact with the Eastern Wing was cut off suddenly, and the Western Wing was convinced they were being tested. The emissary must already be here, watching them, reporting back to his superiors. The Western Wing has a bit of an inferiority complex, you see, and they were positive, *positive*, that the Eastern Wing was intent on taking an accurate measure of their worthiness before teaming up with them again. For a long time they were unsure what to do, other than go about their general operations with a renewed dedication to excellence. But one day, not too long ago, Luther Ado had an idea. What better way to prove their worthiness, their efficiency, their capability, than to *expose* the emissary?"

The fog in my brain, despite the flurry of Le Monde's exposition, was dissipating further. It was a thin chicken noodle, now. "I arrived here seven months ago," I whispered.

"*Précisément*. They rapidly pegged you as the clandestine emissary. The Award ceremony was designed to 'expose' you; the Award, the handshake, the code, it's all legend within the conspiracy. If you were the emissary you would have known what was occurring, and you would have played along. But you did not, so how could you be the emissary?

"Most of them wanted to kill you straight away — remember, they believe the true emissary is still watching and reporting on their every move — but Humphreys took it into his own hands. He invented a test of his own. Every Eastern Winger knows that Everlasting House is the seat of the Western Wing. He would offer you the House — to the emissary that would be incontrovertible proof of the Western Wing's intentions. But this offer, too, you refused.

"The consensus was that you could *not* be the emissary. That they had made a ghastly error. The only way to reconcile that error was to do away with you, quickly and quietly."

Le Monde saw the fifth question in my eyes.

"It would be most uncharacteristic if it were them that poisoned Tara Fury. She is a direct descendant of William Cranston — his granddaughter."

And the sixth.

"I do not know if she is involved, Miles. Her mother — William's daughter — parted company with her siblings at a young age. In effect she renounced THE UNKNOWN. If she was not a relative she would not have been allowed to live. It is possible, though unlikely, that Tara is as ignorant of the conspiracy as you were, before this all began."

The seventh.

"Peter Cranston is a mystery, as well. I have found no concrete evidence that he is involved, but he has won that Award sixteen times, and he *is* Davis Cranston's son. Tara

Fury's mother was very much an exception — if you are a member of that family, you are a member of THE UNKNOWN."

And lastly, the eighth.

"Whether they poisoned *you*? A question mark, but not a large one. There is no question that they lured you to the golf course to kill you, and that they sent an assassin to your apartment. The message is clear: they will not give up until they *have* killed you, Miles, however long it takes. The best thing for you is to leave, right away. Go to an island in the South Pacific, go to a village in Africa, go somewhere out of the way. Change your name, live in peace. Leave THE UNKNOWN to the professionals."

I stared at him stupidly. I was like a blindsided press secretary. The president did *what?* With *who?* In the back seat of *where?* I had been given too much information in too short a space of time, and I couldn't process it all. I could only take it in one tidbit at a time, and the one overwhelming tidbit that consumed me more than any other was that while THE UNKNOWN might have been a massive conspiracy of the powerful and influential, it had chosen the wrong guy to mess with when it had chosen Miles Jeffrey Hudson—

"Miles?"

"Hmm?"

"You're shivering."

"Well, it *is* cold down here."

"It is okay to be afraid. I could not blame you if you were."

"I'm not afraid, I just need a jacket."

"I would offer you my robe, but I still need it, I'm afraid. —Not afraid in the way you are, that is, but afraid in the regretful sense."

I did my best to present a reasonable facsimile of a person who was in control of his bodily functions. "I am *not* afraid," I said, as forcefully as a person can when his teeth are chattering.

But Le Monde was not listening to me. He was listening to Luther Ado, who was wrapping up his address. The black robes burst into a final cacophony of applause.

Le Monde turned back to me. "Must go," he said, replacing his hood. "Remember my advice. And best of luck."

A blur of motion, and he was gone.

CHAPTER XVIII
RULES

ADO'S BRIGADES, WHIPPED INTO A FURY BY HIS DEMAGOGUERY, quick-stepped out of the cavern, as orderly as parochial school students, single-filing through a slender doorway to the right of the obsidian stage. I was appalled that these people could be so sheepishly subservient — I recognized as he passed by the alcove Professor of Chemistry Yuri Zelikov, a Ukrainian immigrant with whom I'd had many a discussion, a man with as independent a mind as ever I'd known (Planck's Constant was, to him, a postulate), and yet here he was, blithely following THE UNKNOWN's party line. The conduct of these people — Yuri, Herman Baumgartner, Rachel Gutierrez, Walter Hendricks, each of whom I'd recognized in their robes and hoods — was so much at odds with what I knew of them that I could almost accept that the conspiracy recruited its membership by blackmail, or other coercive means. But if the conspiracy was as large as Le Monde alleged, their membership had to be, at least for the most part, voluntary.

When the cavern was at last emptied, I whistled at Flynn.

"Is that you, old rug?"

"Who else would it be?"

"I don't know. That sounded more like a bird to me."

"A bird? This far underground?"

"A bat, then. Don't they sound like birds? —No, they don't, do they...but it could be a hybrid, a bat-bird of some kind. They *are* discovering new species every day—"

I ignored him. "We have to follow them, Flynn, find out what their plan is—"

Just then, however, as if in answer to my ingenious proposal, a loud *thud* resounded across the cavern floor. The doorway through which the black robes had exited had been closed.

"There's still time—" I started, but again as if in answer to my very words, a sequence of metallic sounds followed from behind the door. A section of the craggy wall slid down and neatly fell into place, covering the door completely.

"Well, crap," I said to myself.

"That's that, then," said Flynn from above. "I suggest we make haste while we can."

Part of me was disappointed that I would not have the opportunity to investigate further, but another part of me was equally delighted that it would get to go on breathing. I turned toward the wall, hoping that they wouldn't douse the lights, which I needed in order to see the rugged outcroppings I planned to use as hand- and footholds. I jumped and, despite the injury to my back and despite having prolifically avoided exercise of any sort, I was nimble as a tomcat scampering up that wall. Going up against THE UNKNOWN may have awakened in me previously unknown courage and tenacity, but I wasn't about to be left behind in a spooky underground cavern with nothing but a measly flashlight and some matches.

The lights shut off just as I took hold of Flynn's outstretched arms. He pulled, I pushed, and with a grunt I was back up on the ledge.

Flynn thumbed his flashlight directly into my face. "What were you doing all that time? You were down there almost fifteen minutes, old nut! And I'll swear I saw you dialoguing with one of those black-robed yahoos!"

I batted the flashlight away. "I was dialoguing, but I'll fill you in later — let's get out of here, *tout suite.*"

For the first time since this all began, I had some notion of what was taking place, and I had some notion of what to do about it: get to Chauncey and have him procure a search warrant for Everlasting House. He might find nothing, but he might also find a closet full of black robes, which, while not exactly illegal, was definitely *weird.* Weird enough to warrant further investigation, which might find concrete proof of THE UNKNOWN.

Flynn and I retraced our steps through the passage to the library. Flynn tromped about where the torch had fallen, hoping to hit the shelf-door's trigger to close it behind us. I put up my hand to have him hold off a moment, for I had spied a detail I had not spied before: the reverse sides of the shelves were disguised as craggy rock, just as was the steel door on the other side of the room. This meant that, when the shelf-door was shut, an observer on the opposite side would see nothing but stone — as if the original tunnelers had dug to that point, then stopped. This raised the possibility that the conspirators were unaware of the library — still, *someone* had been reading that diary lately, and *someone* had marked those cities on the globe.

I picked up the diary and made certain that both Tara's and my birth certificates were still inside. "Let's go," I said.

"You're taking that with you?" asked Flynn.

"Yes, I am."

"But why?"

"Because it's *my* birth certificate."

"Then take *it*, but not the whole book! They'll know we've been here!"

"So? What are they going to do? Try to kill me?"

"Aren't you the one who said we should leave no trace of our infiltration?"

"That was before."

"Before what?"

"Before I changed my mind."

"What made you change your mind?"

"Believe it or not, the handsomest man I ever saw."

"Oh," said Flynn levelly, as if believing it took little to no effort.

"That didn't come out quite the way I intended," I said.

"No worries," said Flynn, awkward and disjointed. "Let's just get going, shall we?"

Flynn had misunderstood my meaning, but that didn't mean my meaning was any less true: I had changed. At some point during Le Monde's dissertation, a switch had gone off in my mind — prior to meeting him my dander had been up, but after hearing what he'd had to say, everything about me, if you'll pardon the expression, was up. Le Monde, without intending to, had made it as straightforward to me as could be: THE UNKNOWN needed the light of day shone on it; THE UNKNOWN needed to be destroyed; THE UNKNOWN needed to be *stopped*.

And while Jacques Le Monde might be the man to stop it in George Town, Grand Cayman, there was no escaping the fact that I was the man to stop it in Constant, California.

Still, I was hopeful — if that's the word — which it isn't — that a climax was fast approaching. According to Le Monde THE UNKNOWN was up to something, and if it wasn't stopped soon, it wouldn't be stopped at all. One way or another, I had the sense that my travails were nearing an end.

In this, as you can see by the number of pages you still have to read, I was horribly mistaken.

*   *   *

Flynn relit the fallen torch and reinstalled it in its sconce and then we took our leave of the library, shutting the hatch firmly behind us as we went. Neither of us was looking forward to climbing the spiral stairway, but there was no use delaying the inevitable (though we did try, with a few seconds of small talk), so I took the lead and started up.

I hadn't taken three steps before my legs started to cramp. I couldn't blame them, after the ordeals I'd subjected them to. But they struggled valiantly on, while I did their moaning for them. Behind and below me, similar noises emanated from Flynn — we were like two ghosts who just want to go home and get some sleep.

At length — one Astronomical Unit, I believe — we saw bright light that could only come from the noontime sun. We sped our pace. Emerging from the hole, we stood once more on the east lawn of Everlasting House. After securing the storm doors, and their rusted lock, we ran for Lasting Lake, not pausing even for a moment to rest our weary limbs.

As we ran I heard something, but at first I thought it was a trick of my imagination.

"Dokkkturr Hudddd ssssunnnn...Dokkkkkturrrr...."

Putting the syllables together I came up with "Doktur Hudsun," which, it didn't take me long to realize, was, phonetically, my name.

I stopped running and turned around. Jogging toward us, from the direction of the House, was Officer Gerald.

Had he been spying on us again? Had he been shadowing us in the library, and on the ledge? Had he seen what we'd seen? Was it all over?

Of course not. You're barely a page further along.

"Dr. Hudson! Mr. Flynn!" Officer Gerald sprinted right up next to us. He was panting hard, though from what I could tell he hadn't been running for more than ten seconds, and not even at top speed. Constant's finest, indeed.

"I'm sorry to say," he said without sounding sorry, "I have warrants for both of your arrests."

My reaction to this news may be suitably expressed as nonplused multiplied by flummoxed. "Why?" I demanded. "What did *we* do?"

He reached into his coat and lifted two folded documents from an inner pocket. He handed one to me and one to Flynn.

"You trespassed, you broke and entered, and you burgled."

Civility was all that kept me from tearing the warrant to pieces in front of his face. Civility and, I suppose, a fear that doing so would add a charge of willful destruction of government property to the list of charges.

"This is ridiculous!" I protested.

"Have you any idea what we witnessed down there?" asked Flynn. "A 'brave new world'! A gaggle of freaks in black robes, plotting murder and mayhem and world domination!"

"Gerald, it's a global conspiracy—"

Officer Gerald cut me off with a shake of his head. "I sympathize with you, gentlemen, truly I do. But you *were* trespassing, and you *did* break and enter, and" — he plucked the diary from my hand — "you *did* burgle." He shrugged. "I *have* to arrest you. Rules are rules."

CHAPTER XIX
DUH JUDGE

GERALD HANDCUFFED US, PIOUSLY MAINTAINING THAT IT WAS nothing personal, and led us to his car, a red Dodge which, he explained, the department utilized for undercover work. He hustled us into the back seat, then dashed around to the front seat. He buckled his seatbelt and gunned the engine. Thrown back into the velour by the g-forces, I couldn't sit up straight for a time, and when I could, the first things I saw were the gates of Everlasting House as we roared past.

I was apprehensive, on countless fronts. Was it THE UN-KNOWN, through Dr. Humphreys, who had called the police? If they knew we were on their property, why had they bothered with the police? Why not finish us themselves? Or was this their way of "legitimately" silencing us? And how had they known we were there in the first place?

Or, was it possible that Gerald, perhaps on the prompting of Tara, or Chauncey, was acting for our benefit — rescuing us from the enemy's lair? But how would any of them have known where we were, and what we were doing, in the first place?

I also found myself thinking of Captain Queeg. Had I unthinkingly put him and his sons in harm's way? How long would the *Zuider Zee* rest at anchor within sight of Everlasting House? I didn't doubt his ability to take care of himself, but neither did I doubt his ability to hold a grudge against the guy who'd left him with his engine idling thirty feet offshore as hour after hour drifted by like so much flotsam.

I prayed that, whatever else befall me, I not again meet up with Queeg in a dark alley. Or, for that matter, a clean, well-lighted alley.

*   *   *

In my seven months in the incorporated city of Constant, the Courthouse had never much weighed on my mind. Located next to City Hall, it shared its neighbor's bland 50's architecture and faded gray paint job — simply not a scene to command one's visual respect.

But it commanded my visual respect now, all right, just the way the *place de la Revolution* commanded Marie Antoinette's. The building's face became a human face, with windows for eyes and curtains for slanting eyelids, the Great Seal of the County of Constant for a nose, marble steps for evilly smirking teeth...Officer Gerald, with a resigned "Following orders, folks" (studiously applying the lesson of Nuremberg) ushered us straightaway into the mouth of this foul beast.

This, then, was *not* a scheme to spirit us safely from the bad guys' hideout. We actually were under arrest: booked, fingerprinted, mug-shotted, dispossessed of our shoes, belts, and the contents of our pockets, and escorted to a cell in the Courthouse basement. I refused the offer of a civil defense attorney — after hearing our story, what counselor could argue our case with a straight face? — and I refused the obligatory phone call.

I could have telephoned Tara, but what on earth would I have said to her? "Your uncle may be involved in a criminal conspiracy that stretches from Albuquerque to Antarctica, and by the way, I found your birth certificate, along with mine, in a hidden underground library next to a cavern where almost all of my colleagues were dressed up like druids and chanting like snake handlers at the Pentecost."

No, I thought, there was no sense in calling Tara. We'd get out of jail in less time than it would take for me to explain why we were *in* jail.

"I'll speak to the judge right away," Gerald said. "We'll try to get you arraigned as soon as possible. Bail shouldn't be too high, this is your first offense."

"Gerald," I said, "Gerald, listen to me. Search Everlasting House. You'll find a cellar, a cave — Flynn and I can both testify that we saw a group of maniacs down there! A conspiracy to take over the world! You have to believe me! You have to believe *us!*"

"Dr. Hudson, even if I did believe you, I couldn't search a historical House like that without *very* convincing probable cause. The judge is a real stickler."

"Then let us talk to the judge!"

"I said I'd try to get you arraigned as soon as possible, didn't I? Even that's pushing things on my part. Judge Severe is a busy man."

"Sevier?" asked Flynn. "French? S-e-v-i-e-r?"

"No," said Gerald. "Anglo-Saxon. S-e-v-e-r-e."

*   *   *

Sitting there on a bunk with springs like cardboard tubes, I recounted to Flynn the sensational disclosures Le Monde had provided, back in the cave beneath Everlasting House. Flynn's ears pricked up at the first mention of Le Monde—

"You've heard of him?" I asked.

"*Bien sur,*" answered Flynn reverently.

"When you went to France?"

"No, when I was surveying special intelligence apparatus." His voice turned star struck. "Le Monde is a god, you know. He was the first man to infiltrate the Red Revolution. And he single-handedly brought down D.E.S.T.R.U.C.T.!"

"What's D.E.S.T.R.U.C.T.?"

"The Directorate for Evil, Sanctioned Totally with Regard to Unleashing Complete Terror."

"Flynn, that doesn't even make sense."

"He's a *god*," repeated Flynn. "And I was — what? — ten, fifteen feet away from him?"

The mere fact that Le Monde was investigating the conspiracy did far more to solidify the threat of the conspiracy in Flynn's mind than did my conveying to Flynn Le Monde's detailing of the extent of that threat. When I told him of Le Monde's final advice to me, his expression became grave.

"I'm no coward, old horn, but if Jacques Le Monde cautioned *me* to skedaddle, I'd have to give it serious contemplation. And I'd be doing that serious contemplating as I was skedaddling."

"He *was* cautioning you, Flynn, when he cautioned me. You're as deep into this as I am, now. They'll be after you just as doggedly as they're after me. With any luck just as incompetently, too."

Flynn ran his palm along his mouth, and chin. He exhaled a loud breath. "Well, old friend — *you're* not skedaddling, are you?"

"No, but that doesn't mean you shouldn't, or can't."

"I'm staying. Don't try to talk me out of it."

I smiled. "Wouldn't dream of it, Flynn."

He gave me a funny look that — while I may have misinterpreted — seemed to indicate that a nominal attempt at talking him out of it would not have gone unappreciated.

I leaned back against the bars. My mind was a swirling maelstrom of unbidden thoughts colliding against one another. I stuck my head into the sunlight shining through the barred window and looked up into the sky. What a beautiful day, I thought, to be arrested. I sat back down on the bunk and let my shoulders fall against the cement wall. I wished I had my notebook, so that I could update it with my most recent misadventures—

I wasn't aware I had gone to sleep until I was awakened by the rickety clacking of the cell door sliding open.

"Judge had an unexpected opening in his schedule," Gerald informed us. "You're on in five minutes."

*   *   *

The courtroom suited the name of its judge. One window glared down from high above him like a stained glass window shining down on John Brown, whom, in fact, Judge Severe favored. His eyes were plunged deep in their sockets, his chin was wide as his neck, and his hair, combed straight back, towered imperiously over all. His stare was that of the prophet Nathan.

The bailiff, who was so nondescript that when he began talking I thought there was someone trapped in the crawlspace between walls, read the case and passed the proceedings to the judge.

"What plead you?" he asked.

The judge's voice did not match his appearance. In order for his voice to have matched his appearance, he would have had to have been three feet tall and claiming to represent the Lollypop Guild.

"Your honor," I said, "the charges are true, but there were *extremely* mitigating circumstances, not the least of which was my trying to prevent my own murder!"

The judge lowered his head, chuckling. "You're going to fight this, are you, Hudson? Okay. Fine. Let's cut to the chase. The only recording device in this room is the court reporter, who, you'll notice, has stopped typing. She and the bailiff are in the same boat I am, that boat being that our pay-checks are cashed at the First National Bank of THE UNKNOWN. Now I know you're not independently wealthy, but maybe your friend there is. You'd better hope so, anyway, because if he's not, you'll never afford what it takes to bribe all three of us."

He paused, and smiled amiably, expecting our reply.

"I have money," said Flynn.

I frowned at him. "No you don't," I whispered harshly.

"Yes I do."

"*They* don't need to know that, Flynn."

"Not the nest-egg, Miles. I would *never* touch the nest-egg. I have extra money."

"'Extra' money?"

"From Vegas."

"You told me you lost money on that trip."

"I didn't want you to feel you were the only one."

"How much did you win?"

"A fair bit. Gambling is a simple matter of playing the odds and knowing when to quit."

"Hate to interrupt you two lovebirds," said Judge Severe, "but how much money do you *have*, Mr. Flynn?"

"How much do you want?" retorted Flynn.

The judge looked at the bailiff, and at the court reporter. Their faces were blank — and so, I feared, would have to be check that bought them off.

"They *really* want you guys gone," said the judge. "Freedom'll cost you fifty."

The bailiff and the court reporter cast him uneasy glances.

"That's thirty for me, ten for each of you. —Don't start with me. You're not the ones who have to explain how the prisoners escaped, you're not the ones with your feet to the fire. You're lucky I cut you in at all!"

"—Excuse me, your honor," said Flynn, "but did you say fifty dollars?"

The judge burst into horselaughs, and the bailiff fought a snicker. The court reporter, though, faced front stolidly, her fingers poised above the keys. I admired her professionalism, even as I decried her involvement in a homicidal conspiracy.

Judge Severe tittered, "Fifty bucks? To deliver you from THE UNKNOWN? Are you *nuts?* Add a few zeros, son! I'm talkin' eight figures here!"

Flynn's eyes narrowed. Eight is a larger number than two, particularly with regard to decimal places.

"*Fifty million?*" I blurted out, having done the math in my head. "*Fifty million dollars?*"

"That's right, son!"

My ire, not for the first nor the last time during this affair, was aroused. "Who do you think you are, the *Supreme Court?* This isn't *Roe v. Wade!* This is a rinky-dink little burglary charge!   —You didn't win fifty million dollars, did you?" I muttered out of the side of my mouth.

"No," said Flynn. "Gambling isn't *that* simple a matter."

Severe bent forward. "Y'all don't have it, do you? I *knew* it! I knew it the minute I saw you. Big shots with the big bucks, my foot!" His face scrunched up like a stepmother's. "Well, gentlemen, for wasting my time — I'm throwing the book at you! No bail. No trial. I'm not only your judge — I'm your jury! And — yes, gentlemen — I am also your executioner! I hereby sentence both of you to—"

The doors to the courtroom sprang open. A man shot through and skidded to a stop on the slick floor, waving his arms for balance. His open, boyish face radiated cherubic innocence. He smiled like Clark Gable playing Fletcher Christian.

"Who the hell are you?" asked Judge Severe.

"I'm here to save these men," said the man. "I'm Justin Time."

"No, you're too late," said the judge. He returned his gaze to Flynn and me. "Fifty years hard labor, gents, that's your sentence. One year for each mil you didn't have. If *that* doesn't teach you the folly of putting on airs, nothing will."

"Your honor," said the welcome interloper in a marvelously intractable tone, "Justin Time is my name, and I will concur that in this instance it is an exceptionally appropriate moniker, for it seems I have arrived just in time to forestall a dire miscarriage of justice."

"Just exactly who are you, son?" asked the judge.

"A reporter, your honor, and a lawyer."

The judge shuddered. "Ye gods, could you have picked a more atrocious combination of careers? What exactly is your interest in this case?"

"Justice, your honor."

"I thought you said you were a lawyer."

"Very funny, your honor."

"Thank you. But I *am* the judge, and being the judge, you'll have to agree that justice is what I say it is, no?"

"I do not agree that justice is a subjective proposition, no, sir, I do not."

"Where *did* you go to law school, son?"

"I've passed the bar, if that's what concerns you. Personally I am far more concerned about my clients here—"

The judge's snort came out as a hacking cough. "Whoa, son! Your *clients?*" He studied Flynn and me. "You know this snake oil salesman, boys?"

"He's my lawyer," I answered, nudging Flynn in the ribs.

"I've recently taken my business to him as well," said Flynn, prevaricating seamlessly. "I'd heard good things, and I wasn't especially satisfied with my previous firm."

Our lawyer (any port in a storm) smiled a little at our performances. "Your honor, I request dismissal of all charges against these, my clients."

The judge blinked. "What are you, nuts? Are you *all* nuts?"

Justin Time shook his head and expunged a sigh. He looked at the judge, and the bailiff, and the court reporter, and Flynn and I, in turn. He drew in a deep breath and delivered what all concerned understood to be his killer closing. "This is a sham, and a farce, your honor. (I use that title loosely.) These two men are innocent, and you know it. You can dismiss the charges, or you can face the wrath of a fully-prepared attorney who also writes a column for a major metropolitan newspaper."

Judge Severe sat back in his chair and fingered his gavel. "You don't have the *foggiest* what you're doing, Mr. Justin Time. You've put yourself on the same hit list your two supposed 'clients' are on. You're all three *dead!* You're all three *nuts!* Fifty years hard labor's a cakewalk compared to what they'll do to you guys now. You don't mess with them, Mr. Time! You just *don't!*"

"I can take care of myself, sir. So can my clients."

Judge Severe took his gavel up in his hand and played with it nervously. "You got any money, Time? You went to law school, you gotta have some money. I'll tell 'em your clients overpowered the guards, hopped a freight train heading east—" Severe's eyebrows fluttered suggestively.

"You sicken me, sir," said Justin Time.

"Oh, yeah, sure!" said the judge. "Mr. *Lawyer/Reporter!* Why don't you sell used cars, too, then you'd really be respected!"

"Come on," Time said, turning to us. "We're done here."

We followed him down the center aisle, and through the courthouse doors, Judge Severe shouting all the while about insurance actuaries and funeral parlor directors.

CHAPTER XX
TIME IS ON MY SIDE

TIME, SPORTING A PAIR OF WRAPAROUND SUNGLASSES, DROVE A BMW convertible with the top down. He laid his left arm sloppily on the door and steered with his right. For sheer suavity, sheer savoir faire, sheer unadulterated *coolness*, this man outranked everyone of my acquaintance (including even, yes, Jacques Le Monde), and sitting in the passenger seat of that car, breathing the rich, heady 90 mph air, the breeze blowing my hair back like a windsock, I felt as if Justin Time's aura of coolness had expanded to envelop me, as well. I felt cool by association. I felt invincible. I almost stood up in the seat and grabbed hold of the windshield: Patton in his Sherman on the road to Berlin. An irresistible force for which there existed no corresponding immovable object.

Yes, sir, I was riding tall in the turret indeed, until Time began to giggle. There was no particular cause for it, he just started giggling. A high-pitched, staccato, nasal giggle — a giggle not usually heard outside of a Saturday morning cartoon.

The giggle continued as we pushed down the main road that linked Constant to the state highway, twelve miles away. The road ran parallel to the railroad tracks, which worried me a bit, because Severe would be needing a story to tell his superiors to cover his posterior, and the one about the freight train heading east, as we were, was fresh on his mind.

But George S. wouldn't have dwelt on this negative notion, so I didn't, either.

Presently, still rocking with giggles, Time pulled off onto a skinny dirt road that wound a crooked path between two dilapidated wooden fences. Beyond these lay an orchard, its orange trees lined in orderly rows. When the car was out of sight of the main road, Time slowly applied the brakes. We rolled to a stop.

Time twisted in his seat, hanging his right arm over the backrest. He stopped giggling. "Smartly done, eh? If I do say so myself!" He chortled self-satisfactorily.

"Who are you?" asked Flynn from the back seat.

"I'm your lawyer!" said Time, giggling. "—No, really. Who am I? Call me...an emissary." He nodded at the door. "Get out."

The implications of his revelation hit me with a physical force, knocking me back against the seat. "*You're* the emissary?" My voice was hushed. "You're from the Eastern Wing? You're who they thought *I* was?"

"Guilty!" squealed Time.

"But why did you rescue us?"

"Because the Western Wing's a bunch of nincompoops, that's why. Luther's got them worked up into a froth — he's got something up his sleeve, something big, and when he gives them the word he doesn't want them to think about it, he wants them to *do* it. I've been warning my handlers in the Eastern Wing not to come anywhere near these dolts, but everybody's dead-set on putting the hyphen back between the yin and the yang."

"You haven't answered the question," I said. "Why rescue us?"

He giggled. "Mostly just to tweak Luther's nose. And to put my law degree to use, for once. It does also serve the

purpose of informing them, at long last, that the fabled emissary, *c'est moi.*"

"How does it do that?" I asked.

"They'll find out I'm not your lawyer, sooner or later,
and who besides an untouchable co-conspirator would defy
THE UNKNOWN that brazenly?"

He, literally, tee-heed.

"You realize you're giving their intellectual reasoning
the benefit of the doubt," I said.

"I grant you. But they'll figure it out, eventually."

"Then we're nothing but pawns in your little chess
match with Luther Ado."

"That's a fair characterization," declared Time. "But you
don't deserve fifty years' hard labor, either. The Western
Wing is desperate to prove itself — they're going way overboard. We in the East are a more mellow bunch. We sit back,
take things in, make informed, intelligent decisions. If you'd
done what you're doing here in Constant in, say, Pittsburgh?
We'd have had you committed to an asylum for a year or two.
For the rest of your life your talk of a global conspiracy would
be considered the mindless babble of a kook."

Flynn flared, "We're not stopping, Time — if that's your
real name" — Time grinned — "not till we've brought down
your conspiracy."

Time clucked his tongue. "Odds aren't good. Sixty million of us, two of you."

Sixty million? Surely he was exaggerating. Surely.
There couldn't be *sixty million* of them, could there?

I put on a brave face, though whether because there
couldn't be sixty million of them, or because there *were* sixty
million of them, I could not say.

"I will admit," said Time, "that here in Constant, considering who you're up against, the odds are about even." He smiled. "Still, I wouldn't bet on you."

I reached into my shirt pocket. "What do you know about these?" I asked. "We found them in Everlasting House."

He gave the birth certificates a once-over. "You and Miss Fury, eh? Huh. Interesting."

"Interesting?"

"I'm not about to tell you what these mean, not least because I don't know. I have an idea, but all it is is an idea. I will tell you this," he said, his voice suddenly that of Vincent Price: "These do not bode well."

"Is Tara a collaborator? Is she in the Eastern Wing?"

He frowned. "No. Goodness, no. Have I been giving *your* intellectual reasoning the benefit of the doubt? What on earth gave you the idea that Tara's in on this? She's a wild card — working to re-fuse the two factions of her family, but in the dark as to what her family really is, or why it broke apart in the first place."

"Who's trying to kill her?"

"Search me."

"And Peter? Is he in the Western Wing?"

"Peter Cranston? Let me put it this way: *sixteen* Professor Of The Month Awards. To the Western Wing that's like sixteen Medals of Honor. You don't come by those puppies by accident."

"I did," I said miserably.

He laughed and gave me back the certificates. "I applaud your spunk, Dr. Hudson, Mr. Flynn. And I'll give you a chance to put it to use. You're walking back to Constant."

"But it's—" I began, intending to end with, "at least five miles back to Constant," but stopped myself in the middle.

As Sigmund Freud once wrote, there's no sense arguing with a cackling megalomaniac.

I flapped a hand at Flynn, waving him out of the car, following after myself. I turned back as I swept shut the door, meaning to ask Time about Dr. Humphreys' role in all of this, but it was too late.

He was yelling "So long!" while turning the ignition. The engine growled. The tires spat up dust. The BMW hung motionless for a moment, its wheels digging for traction, and then they caught. The car rocketed away in a dirty brown cloud that obliterated our view of the sunset into which Justin Time sped.

CHAPTER XXI
TRUST

THE SUN SET QUICKLY AND DARKNESS FELL. THE MOON WAS BUT A quarter full, providing little light by which to see our way. I had thought we were only a mile or so off the main road, but after walking for an hour and still not reaching it, I decided that making the original trip in the BMW must have skewed my perceptions of time and space. We plodded onward through the orange grove, espying no sign of the main road.

After a while Flynn moved toward the right-side fence, over which hung a drooping branch dripping with oranges. He reached up and pulled down an orange, then clawed his fingers into it as we walked on.

"You're just going to eat that?" I asked.

"No, I thought I'd peel it and use it as a compass," replied Flynn acidly. "Of course I'm going to eat it! What else would I do with it?"

I had a few choice suggestions, but I kept them to myself. "What I mean is, it's straight off the tree. They could have sprayed that orchard with...I dunno, malathion or something."

"Malathion? What's malathion?"

Flynn had apparently never gone through an agricultural phase.

"It's an insecticide," I told him. "Like DDT."

"DDT was banned long ago," he said with a wave of his hand. "This orange is perfectly good." He popped a wedge of it into his mouth.

"DDT isn't the only insecticide ever used by the human race," I elucidated patiently. "There are hundreds of others, and just because they're safe by the time the fruit gets to market doesn't mean they're safe while the fruit is still on the tree."

Flynn popped another wedge. "Well, I'm not dead yet," he said, the sarcasm in his voice harsh and unmistakable. "Do let me know if I fall over and lapse into convulsions, won't you?"

We walked on in silence. Flynn was silent because he was enjoying his orange. I was silent because I had had two insights.

My first insight was that Flynn was upset with me, and not merely because I had impinged on his enjoyment of his orange. He was upset with me because I had dared to question the trustworthiness of Peter and Tara. Despite the heaping amounts of evidence he'd received to the contrary recently, Flynn's world was and would always remain a simple one. A friend was a friend and an enemy was an enemy. Peter and Tara were friends — we'd gotten drunk together, which in Flynn's book made them all but family — and THE UNKNOWN was the enemy. To confuse one for the other was an unforgivable heresy.

My second insight was that that orange of his looked darn tasty.

*   *   *

"Flynn," said I, some minutes later, "I have received a series of shocks during the past few days. My life has been turned upside down. It can never return to what it was before. People I knew and believed in and thought of as friends have turned out to be members of an organization devoted to evil. I honestly feel as if there's no one left I can trust."

Flynn recoiled, deeply hurt. "No one, old rum?"

"Flynn," I said, spitting out a rind from my plucked orange, "I would trust you with my life. You know that. I'm not talking about you. I'm talking about every single other person in the entire world. For God's sake, they had my *birth certificate!* You know what that means? My own parents may not be who I think they are!"

"You look just like your father, old wart. Not much chance he didn't provide the Y chromosome, at least."

"I don't mean they aren't my biological parents, I mean they might be mixed up in this conspiracy! If I can't trust my own parents, how can I trust anyone?"

Flynn mulled this over. "I see your point," he said.

"Our first job," I said, "is to stop whatever Luther Ado has planned for the Western Wing here in Constant. My second job — which you don't have to be a part of if you don't want to — is to find out the truth about that birth certificate."

"Miles," said Flynn, grabbing me by the shoulders, "I want you to remember one thing: I am on your side. You can trust me. I have never lied to you, and I will never lie to you. When I tell you something, you may rest assured without reservation that *it is the truth.* —What's the matter?"

"My stomach." I winced. "I don't think that orange I picked is sitting well."

Flynn removed his arms from my shoulders. "Well, I feel fine. You should have taken your orange from the same tree I did. If only you'd trusted me, old bones!"

CHAPTER XXII
Q.E.D.

I WAS HIGH AND FLYNN WAS LOW AS WE KICKED IN THE DOOR TO my apartment. We didn't have guns, of course, but we did have two short heavy sticks we'd found on our trek through the woodlands. Flynn, overplaying his part, dove into the room and rolled across the floor, shrieking like a Chinese martial artist, coming up at the ready on his feet, his stick weaving terse, intricate patterns in the air.* I simply leapt into the room, stick held high.

Tara and Peter had been sitting on the sofa, but Tara jumped up, dually startled by our showboating entrance and by Peter's spilling his drink right in her lap, after which Peter clutched his heart and took a number of whale-like gulps.

"Good Lord, what are you doing?" he hoarsed.

Flynn flew toward Peter, dancing about him in a blur. When he disengaged, Peter's arms were so entangled in the stick that he looked like a piece of living Celtic jewelry.

"Good Lord, what are you doing?" repeated Peter, evincing a certain amount of stress.

Flynn snarled, "You don't win the Professor Of The Month Award sixteen times by accident, Dr. Cranston!"

---

* And nine years since his Bruce Lee phase — indicating Flynn did retain *some* scraps of the vast smorgasbord of knowledge he cycled through.

Apparently my talk with Flynn had awakened in him the concept of *distrust* — and as usual, Flynn had embraced the new concept with wild abandon.

"Miles," asked Tara, "what's going on? When we woke up you were gone, and Officer Gerald said we weren't allowed to leave. We've been so worried—"

"Yes," I said slyly. "Gerald's in on it, too, isn't he, Peter?"

Peter goggled in my direction. "In on *what*, Miles?"

Had I not seen Peter's performance in the spring production of *Richard III*, I would have been struck by the sincerity of his dissembling.

"In on *it*, Peter. THE UNKNOWN — the conspiracy. You're in it up to your gills. *Sixteen times*, Peter — how many people have you helped bury in your never-ending quest for power?"

"My never-ending quest for power? I'm a professor at a college of 1500 students!"

"What better cover? Who would ever suspect you? Or any of your bloodthirsty colleagues?"

"Miles, he's my uncle, he would never—"

"Tara, please. —What was your assignment, Peter? Keep an eye on us? Gently steer us in the wrong direction with preposterous theories about vindictive gypsies? "

Peter, struggling with the stick, appeared wounded. "It wasn't preposterous. Unlikely — improbable — but not preposterous."

This was miles beyond *Richard III*. This was Sir Laurence in *Othello*. Either Peter had been rehearsing twelve hours a day or this was not a performance at all.

"Peter — the Award isn't given for being a wonderful professor, it's given for service to the cause. Service to the conspiracy! How have you won it sixteen times if not for phenomenal service to the conspiracy?"

"*What* conspiracy, Miles?"

Even Sir Larry couldn't have faked the dumb expression that covered Peter's face. He was genuinely mystified.

I paused and reconsidered. "It is true that neither Le Monde nor Time implicated you directly..."

"Le Monde? Time? Miles, what *are* you talking about?"

"Still," I said, more to myself to Peter, "why would the Western Wing honor you so lavishly? *Sixteen* Professor of the Month Awards?"

Peter said, "I am a highly respected lecturer, author of over two dozen works on—"

"Don't trust him," warned Flynn. "Writers are liars by nature."*

I knelt in front of Peter. "Give me one good reason to trust you," I said. "All I need is one."

Peter's face fell into a mélange of expressions, from disorientation to exasperation to rumination, with stops at every emotion in-between. The only sounds that came out of his mouth were guttural *tchs* and *hffs* — the sounds of a man frantically attempting to think of one thing to say — just *one* thing — and coming up one thing short.

If he'd been guilty, I figured, words would have flowed from him like milk and honey.

"Remove the stick," I said to Flynn.

Flynn shot me a glance that told me that whatever happened next was *my* responsibility. Then with one swift motion and a sudden "Hai-ya!", he yanked the stick out from Peter's arms.

Peter stood for a moment in the same pose before realizing that the stick was gone and he could move freely. He

---

* True.

shook his arms to regain circulation. "Miles, what the devil's going on?"

I blew a large breath through my lips. "Peter, a lot is happening, a lot *has* happened, that you know as much about as the cavemen knew about particle physics. Constant College is a college, but it's also the seat of a large conspiracy. You and I may be the only faculty not involved in it."

With regard to dumb expressions, Peter topped himself.

I went on. "Flynn and I are in great peril. This is the last place we should have come, especially if Gerald was—"

With regard to dumb expressions, I topped Peter.

"Yes, Miles?" said Tara. Her face had transformed: from a wide-eyed guileless naiveté to a Machiavellian resolve.

"*Stay where you are!*" shouted Officer Gerald from the doorway. He held a snub-nosed .38 in his right hand. He took a step in and swung the door shut behind him. "How did you get back here, Dr. Hudson? The judge said you were on a freight train—"

"Heading east, yes. Severe is a crook, Gerald. His paycheck's drawn on the First National Bank of THE UNKNOWN."

Gerald's gun did not waver, and as it was pointed squarely at me, I spoke quickly. "Gerald — who was it who alerted you that Flynn and I were at Everlasting House?"

The gun wavered not. "I'll ask the questions, Dr. Hudson. Do you have any solid proof that Judge Severe is dirty?"

Ignoring the commands of a person who is holding a gun on you is not easy, but I'm proud to say that, after two or three seconds of hesitation,* I did so. "Officer, please answer that one question and then I'll answer your questions to your heart's content. Who tipped you off?"

---

* Or ten or fifteen — time becomes elastic, under these circumstances.

Gerald debated inwardly, and it showed outwardly. After a lengthy period he said, "It was an anonymous phone tip."

"Male or female?"

"That's two questions, Dr. Hudson—"

"Male or female?" I insisted, my voice moderately above the conversational level.

"And you said he was a pushover," Tara said to Peter. An edge had entered her voice. An edge had entered her *personality*.

Gerald glowered at me. "Female," he said. "I have a hunch it was Mrs. Humphreys. She's something of a wallflower. Seeing the two of you prowling around her shrubbery must have scared the wits out of her."

"But you can't say for certain who it was, can you?" I pressed him. "Only that the voice was female."

Gerald was simmering. I knew I was pushing him too far, and I knew he was holding a gun on me, but I had to make him *see*.

He said, "No, Dr. Hudson, I can't say for certain. If I could say for certain I'd stop calling it an 'anonymous' phone tip."

I nodded. A conclusion, a definite conclusion, intuited by my own brain, was within my grasp. It hadn't been stumbled upon, it hadn't been disclosed to me by a third party — this conclusion was mine, all mine. And it was kind of important, too.

"Gerald — go to your surveillance room, disconnect your equipment, pack it up, get it out of there. Then use your handcuffs to lock Tara to the radiator, or whatever you can find. Make sure she can't escape."

Dumb expressions were certainly the order of the day. If not for me, it would have been unanimous throughout the room.

"Why?" asked Gerald.

"Miles, old bag?" asked Flynn.

"You will not touch my niece," declared Peter.

"What have *I* done?" quoth Tara, a bit too *mea culpa* to be genuine.

I stood undaunted. "To begin with, *you* called Gerald. When you awoke and found that Flynn and I were gone, you knew where we'd gone — but you had no way of communicating with your cohorts. You couldn't leave, your uncle wouldn't have let you. So you devised an ingenious plot: enlist the aid of the legitimate authorities. You telephoned Officer Gerald—"

"No she didn't!" objected Peter. "She didn't use the phone this morning. I would have seen her."

"Gerald, what time did the call come through?"

"Around eleven."

"Peter, did you shower this morning?"

"Of course I did, I'm not a philistine—"

"At what time?"

"After brunch, around eleven...o'...clock..."

"*Quod erat demonstrandum,*" I said victoriously (and pretentiously). "While you were in the shower Tara called Gerald, disguising her voice, and Gerald assumed it was Mrs. Humphreys. Her plan was a stunning success."

Peter sat down, shellshocked. "Tara — is this true?"

Tara smiled. I was afraid she might start giggling, but she didn't. "Of course it's true, you gargantuan jackass."

The nose of Gerald's .38 wavered at last, shifting toward Tara.

"Tara?" Peter's voice, pitiable and wretched, could barely sustain itself. He gazed at his niece through tear-rimmed eyes.

"There *is* a conspiracy?" said Gerald, skepticism still running rampant through his voice. "At the *college?*"

"It's everywhere," I said, recognizing how similar my rhetoric was to Bruce Washington's. Troubling, to be sure, to bear *any* similarity to Bruce Washington, but the man had been right about THE UNKNOWN. And if Bruce Washington's lunatic ravings were to be trusted, then everything I'd ever been taught about how to distinguish sanity from inanity was being called into question. It was like hearing that UFOs were real, that ancient astronauts built the pyramids, and that the earth was flat, all in one Special Report.

I said, "The conspiracy's west coast base is at the college. They've been orchestrating something, some grand design of theirs — we don't know the details. Our real dilemma, Gerald, is that we don't know who to trust. If Judge Severe is with THE UNKNOWN, anyone could be."

Gerald looked at me. "You don't think Chief Detective Super—"

"I don't know about Chauncey, Gerald. That's the trouble. Anyone we talk to, anyone we bring in to help us, could well be one of theirs. *You* could be one of theirs — although if you were, I suspect you'd still be holding the gun on me and not Tara."

"You don't trust me?" asked Gerald, using the same indignant tone of voice that Flynn had used when he felt I was questioning his credibility.

"I trust you enough to let you be the one holding the gun," I said, a sentence that in retrospect was not among my most well-thought-out. Gerald merely nodded, though, as if this response fully addressed the demands of his self-esteem.

I glanced around. Flynn was absentmindedly twirling his stick in a circle. Peter was staring at the floor, wringing his hands. Tara stood with her arms folded, her smoldering gaze directed at the innermost reaches of my soul. Gerald held his gun on her steadily, watching her from the corner of his eye. We were, unquestionably, a motley crew.

"We're alone," I announced. "We have to stop them, and we'll have to do it alone."

"How?" asked Gerald. "If they're *everywhere*, as you say, I would take it as a given that we *can't* stop them."

I sighed. "We can't destroy them, no. But we can disrupt them. We can ruin Constant College as a base for them."

"And how do we do that?"

I chewed on my lip. "I don't know. But you're a policeman, you must have had training in this sort of thing—"

"In disrupting conspiracies? Sorry, Dr. Hudson, we were too busy studying radio etiquette."

"Old yam," cut in Flynn, "it wouldn't be wise to formulate a plan of action until we've confirmed what *their* plan of action is."

I bit my lip, for Flynn was absolutely right. Once more I could but marvel, for at times Flynn couldn't have identified his own hand in front of his face, but at other times he was able to see clearly through the inkiest of muddles. He denied the former and attributed the latter to his summer in Tibet.

"You're absolutely right," I said. "*That's* our plan of action. To confirm what *their* plan of action is."

Peter said, "Huh?"

"Clear out your surveillance room," I ordered Gerald a second time. "Don't contact Chauncey, don't contact anyone. We're going to give THE UNKNOWN a taste of their own medicine!"

CHAPTER XXIII
THEIR OWN MEDICINE

GERALD SAID "THANKS, BUT NO" TO OUR OFFER TO HELP HIM BOX up the police department's surveillance equipment, expounding that it was "ungodly expensive" and "delicate as a spider's web." Flynn began a discourse on how spider's webs are, proportionally, stronger than steel, and Peter made a remark that this was hogwash, and Gerald said he didn't know about steel, but spider's webs were actually surprisingly strong. Peter asked why he'd called them delicate, then, and Gerald said he was speaking off-the-cuff and wasn't aware that his every utterance would come under such scrutiny. Peter countered that a man should think before he speaks, a maxim I knew from personal experience Peter did not himself follow with stringency.

Observing all of this was Tara, laughing her posterior off.

I broke up the brouhaha and Gerald withdrew, after one last cross-wise glance at Peter, leaving me the revolver. I was taking no chances with Tara. I kept the .38's muzzle trained on her like an owl's eyes on a mouse.

"Miles," she said, her voice languid and sultry, "why do you resist? Do you think you're Winston Churchill? T.E. Lawrence? Fighting against all odds to victory?" She smiled compassionately. "The truth is you're Davy Crockett, or George Custer...and we're Santa Ana...we're the Sioux..."

"I got the analogy a while ago," I said sharply. "No need to go on and on with it."

"If you let me go, Miles, if you simply let me go, if you simply set me free…"

"Yes?"

She shook her head. "No, they'll still kill you."

The urge — who am I kidding, the overpowering *need* — to strike a woman has ne'er been more with me than it was at that moment. Unfortunately, however, my parents raised me better than that.

"If they kill me," I said, holding the pistol even more menacingly than before, "they kill *you*. You're what's known as a hostage."

She bowed her head. "Miles, Miles. You'd never shoot me. You don't have it in you."

"Wanna bet?"

Her eyes locked onto mine. She still wore that condescending smile. "Yeah," she said.

I scowled at her. Okay, so she was right. I'd never shoot her. My parents raised me better than *that*, too. Would their interference in my life never stop?

"Flynn," I growled, "get a rag from the kitchen drawer."

He bounced to his feet.

"What are you going to do?" asked Tara snidely. "*Wipe* me out?"

"Make it terrycloth," I said to Flynn.

*   *   *

I'm sure you're asking yourself what my plan was.

I was asking myself the same question.

"But why," you may ask, "did you say you were going to give THE UNKNOWN a taste of their own medicine if you hadn't worked out *how* you were going to give them a taste of their own medicine?"

Because, I may answer, the adrenaline had been pumping earlier, thundering through my veins at speeds that gave the lie to Einstein's theories, and out of this sodium pentothal-like delirium had come the bravado, the chutzpah, the stones, to deliver a line like "We're going to give THE UNKNOWN a taste of their own medicine." Ordinarily, I assure you, such a line would never cross my mind, much less pass my lips.

Not that the sentiment behind it wasn't genuine — I did want to give THE UNKNOWN a taste of their own medicine, preferably a pharmacy's worth. To do that it would be necessary, as Flynn had said, to uncover Luther Ado's plan, his grand design…but I had about as much idea what might be the specific steps to take to reach this general goal as I would have had if the general goal had been to send a man to the moon. (*Less* idea, in fact — I'd learned quite a bit by osmosis during Flynn's NASA phase.)

But when you've spoken the line "We're going to give THE UNKNOWN a taste of their own medicine" in front of other people, those people, not unfairly, tend to expect you to *have specific steps to take to reach that goal.* In other words, I was discovering, at the ripe old age of 27, exactly what is meant by the phrase "wracking my brain." I had to think of *something.*

This is why I have, for the most part, forgiven myself for what came next.

*   *   *

I laid out my freshly-brainstormed strategy to Gerald and Flynn in the back seat of Flynn's car, a Mercedes he'd bought used in the midst of a Bismarck phase. We were parked one block up from my apartment. Peter and Tara were in the front seat, so we could keep six eyes and one gun on them — Peter frozen with anxiety behind the wheel, Tara making strange noises through the gag that may have been laughter.

These seemed to coincide with what I considered to be the high points of my plan.

"What do you think?" I asked when I was through.

Neither Gerald nor Flynn lifted their eyes from the floor mats.

"Well?"

"Old sin," said Flynn, "you've been under a great deal of stress—"

"You don't like the plan?"

"Let's not go so far as to call it *the* plan," said Gerald. "*A* plan, or *Miles Hudson's* plan, but not *the* plan."

"You've had the same amount of time as I have to develop a proposal, and I don't see you bringing anything to the table!"

"We are not at a board meeting, Miles," said Gerald, as if to a small child, "we are in a war for our very lives." (A raucous burst of...noise...from Tara.) "Careful deliberation would seem to be the order of the day."

"I *did* deliberate carefully!" said I, lying to both them and myself. "What's so bad about my plan? It's unexpected and it's dangerous, but we're already in more danger than a moderate Arab, and the unexpectedness of it is what'll make it work! They'll never see it coming!"

Gerald smoldered. Flynn was beginning to vacillate, I could tell, because he was sitting quietly — always a sign, with him, of brainwave activity.

"When you think about it," he reflected, "what do we have to lose?"

Gerald threw his hands up in the air. "*That's* your argument?" he groaned. "Logic?"

CHAPTER XXIV
THE WORST-LAID PLANS

TO OUR SURPRISE IT WAS DR. HUMPHREYS WHO ANSWERED THE door at Everlasting House, though we didn't find that out until he lay prostrate on the front porch with his arms pinned behind him, his face pressed against the cement, a gun pushed into his temple.

"Wha...what goes on?" he choked out.

I looked at the figure we'd attacked, and noticed for the first time — in our defense, it was a little after eight o'clock, the sky darkening into night — the diminutive frame and the bald head. "Dr. Humphreys?"

"*Miles?*"

"Good Lord, it's Humphreys!" said Flynn.

"Let him up, let him up!" I cried, lifting my knee from the small of his back.

He turned over and gave each of our faces a cursory examination, his expression a mingling of outrage and intense puzzlement. "Miles...thank God you arrived in time! These two brigands had the unmitigated gall to assault me on the doorstep of my very own home!" He started to stand. "You watch them, I'll go and call the police."

"Dr. Humphreys," I said, helping him to his feet (degenerative bone disease, my foot), "you're mistaken. I helped. The *three* of us assaulted you."

The word "confounded" was written on his face in each of the eight languages he purported to speak.

"We thought you were Jenkins," I explained. "Jenkins always answers the door. Even on his days off."

"You thought *I* was Jenkins?"

"Yes."

"Then you meant to assault *Jenkins?*"

"Yes."

He rubbed his forehead. "I'm no nearer an understanding of this incident, Miles. Why in heaven's name would you want to assault Jenkins? And you haven't introduced me to your friends here…"

"This is my best friend Flynn and this is Police Officer Gerald."

"How do you do," said Dr. Humphreys, smiling politely. Then he looked, startled, at Gerald. "Police officer? Has my butler broken the law? Did you come here to arrest him? Is that why the fisticuffs?"

"No, sir," said Gerald. "We — you—" he stammered. "I'd best defer to Dr. Hudson," he said sheepishly.

Dr. Humphreys peered at me. "Miles?"

I took a deep breath. "I had to see you, Dr. Humphreys. It was vital that I give you a message. Jenkins never would have let me inside — that's why the fisticuffs."

Dr. Humphreys bowed his head. "Jenkins has disappeared," he said with sadness. "We've not seen hide nor hair of him since he retired to his bungalow last evening. My wife is half out of her mind with worry!"

She's still half a mind ahead, I thought.

Gerald, in his officious tenor, spoke up. "We appreciate your concern, sir, but we do have a message to deliver."

"Message?" Dr. Humphreys removed his spectacles and set to cleaning them with a handkerchief procured from his breast pocket. "I hesitate to ask what sort of message it may be, that you go to these lengths to deliver it! Couldn't you simply have telephoned?"

"It had to be in person," I said. "It's very important."

"You know, I had the nicest telephone conversation the other day—"

"Dr. Humphreys—"

"Yes?"

"I'd like to shake your hand."

Putting my inspired, well-thought-out plan into action, I held out both hands toward him and crossed them into an X.

Dr. Humphreys' hands stopped moving for a second as he surveyed my attempt to respond, a day after the fact, to his presentation of the Professor Of The Month Award. Then he continued cleaning his glasses, meticulously obliterating from the lenses even the tiniest molecule of dust. He replaced the spectacles on his nose and wrapped the frames around his ears.

"That *is* an important message," he said, his tight smile aimed at me. "Won't you come inside?"

*   *   *

For once, "inside" Everlasting House was not a location you would not want to visit without an ample supply of bread-crumbs; on this occasion "inside" meant the foyer just inside the front door.

"Gee," said Gerald, drinking in the room like a child at a toy store. "I've read about Everlasting House, seen pictures in magazines, but...gee..."

"Neo-Georgian, isn't it?" Flynn asked Dr. Humphreys.

"Why, yes," he replied.

Flynn nodded his head approvingly, but there was a distance in his eyes. His architecture phase had ended at the same time as his relationship with Susan Warner, who'd left him to pursue, of all things, professional ice-skating.

"The message," said Dr. Humphreys, standing before me with dignity, resolve, gravity — three adjectives that, up until that time, should you have mentioned the name Franklin Allen Humphreys, would have fled my mind altogether. "You wish me to pass it on?"

"Yes," I replied. "The season of deceit is passed. The season of reconciliation has begun."

Dr. Humphreys stared at me blankly.

"You — er — you take my meaning?"

"Not in the least," said Dr. Humphreys.

I said, "We have done with the season of lies. We revel in the season of openness."

Dr. Humphreys' face was as vacant as the Bates Motel.

I said, "The mighty fist of THE UNKNOWN has smashed through the corrupting facade of subterfuge."

"Miles, when I taught Kierkegaard I wasn't this obtuse. What is it you're trying to say?"

"Oh, nothing," I said casually. "But you will pass on the message?"

"Certainly," said Dr. Humphreys. "That's what I'm here for. Though I'm still at a loss as to why you couldn't simply telephone."

I folded my arms, secure in the knowledge that my inspired, well-thought-out plan had worked. Gerald and Flynn glared at me, their demeanors expressing their disappointment that the plan they'd been so sure would fail had instead succeeded. And these, I thought contentedly, are my *friends*.

Gerald suddenly stepped forward. "It's imperative, Dr. Humphreys, that THE UNKNOWN understands that this message is proof of Dr. Hudson's *bona fides*."

I signaled in Gerald's direction, a signal the meaning of which could not have been less unambiguous, and that meaning was, "Shut up *shut up!*" but he went right on talking.

"Dr. Hudson's real purpose in being here is to see them. To talk to them. Be sure to tell them, Dr. Humphreys! Be sure they understand!"

I lowered my head. What was Gerald thinking? *Was* Gerald thinking?

Dr. Humphreys eyed us strangely, like a psychic scrutinizing a particularly puzzling aura. I worried that Gerald's unnecessary chattering might have jeopardized what had plainly already been accomplished — Dr. Humphreys had demonstrated that he was not the most stable of persons, and I was afraid that all it would take was one wrong word, one wrong gesture, for him to toss us out on our backsides. Or mow us down with a hidden machine gun.

But then Dr. Humphreys smiled his fraternal smile, abruptly transmuting into host mode. "We have chairs in the library. You may wait there while I'm about my task." He chuckled. "My word...it's been...what?...twenty years?... since I last showed guests to the library. How Jenkins has spoiled us! I wonder where he could be?"

He shuffled into the Everlasting labyrinth, his face screwed up in vexation.

*   *   *

We had left Peter and Tara in the Mercedes on the front drive. Peter — not unlike another who shall remain nameless — had required a certain interval of digestion, a time to concede and accept that what he'd believed his life to be was as near the truth as was your average communist newspaper. When we'd left him he was starting to come out of it, starting to nod his head slowly left to right, right to left, and even to say a word or two, although these words were about as intelligible as those Tara persisted in spitting through her gag. I did get the impression that she might have been trying to tell us something, but I decided to leave her be to struggle against her bonds. Probably she only wanted to laugh at us again anyway, or have fun taking potshots at and poking holes in my plan.

And my plan already bore too much of a resemblance to a cork as it was.

But, like a cork, it was still afloat...the first part, aside from the Humphreys/Jenkins mix-up, had gone smashingly. Dr. Humphreys had, so to speak, taken the bait. Now we would see if Ado and his cronies would bite as well.

Strolling into the library, I instructed Flynn, "Bring in Peter and Tara."

Gerald spoke up. "This is where you've lost me, Dr. Hudson. You intend to deceive THE UNKNOWN into thinking you *are* a member of the conspiracy — and yet you intend to hold Miss Fury hostage! You don't perceive a conflict there?"

I sat down in the largest chair in the room, presumably the chair Dr. Humphreys usually occupied. "I do indeed perceive a conflict, Officer Gerald, but therein, as the Bard wrote, lies the rub. Our coming here — more specifically, *my* coming here — is a development Luther Ado could not have anticipated. A definite, as it were, spanner in the works. It will throw him off-balance, I think you'll agree."

Gerald was unimpressed with my newfound oratorical élan (which appears to be resurfacing even as I recount it). He did something that may have been rolling his eyes and said, "The question is, how long will he *stay* off-balance?"

My smile was smug. "However long, it'll only be longer once I reveal that Tara Fury is a renegade agent, working on her own, toward her own pathological ends."

"But she'll tell them the truth!" exclaimed Gerald.

"Exactly! But *is* it the truth? Or is it Tara who's lying and me who's telling him the truth? I'll use his conspiratorial mindset against him. He can't know for certain whom to trust — and the chance, the slightest possibility, that I *might* be the Eastern emissary will prevent him from harming me. Or any of you."

"Sounds as if we owe you an apology," said Flynn, extending his hand to me, which I shook with bonhomie. "It's ingenious, old tar! Except—"

"Yes?" I said, aware of a sudden sinking feeling.

"What about us? Officer Gerald and myself. And Dr. Cranston, for that matter. How do we fit in?"

I realized that the sinking feeling had nothing to do with what Flynn or Gerald had said. Ignoring it, I forged ahead.

"You came to Constant just weeks after I did, Flynn, and Gerald, you've been on the force only a short while. Ergo, you're the Eastern emissary's dedicated assistants! And Peter? Peter is..."

The sinking feeling now bordered on an attack of vertigo.

"Peter is — a wild card. We don't want this to sound *too* pat, *too* good to be true. Peter stumbled in where he shouldn't have. We're keeping him incarcerated in his own best interests."

My eyes seemed much farther from the ceiling than they'd been when I walked in.

"Don't worry, if Ado tries anything, I'll use my pull as the Eastern emissary to see Peter stays safe — *ahhhh!*"

My scream was like that of a sorority girl who's looked in a mirror on the night of the mixer and discovered a ginormous pimple.

"Very reassuring, Dr. Hudson," said Gerald, deadpan. "If only Dr. Cranston had been here to hear it."

"Something up, old news?" asked Flynn.

Other than that I'd just screamed and curled myself into a fetal position, I can't imagine how such an idea had entered Flynn's head. As if my name were Legion, I babbled, "*The room the room the room! Down down down down!*"

Both Flynn and Gerald gave me a look that said, "Um…what, now?"

"The room!" I sputtered. "The room is going *down!* Can't you feel it?"

Flynn looked at Gerald, and Gerald looked at Flynn. "Do you recall," said Flynn slowly, "my comment regarding stress…?"

"An *elevator room!*" I said breathlessly.

Gerald said, "Dr. Hudson, your mind has snapped. I had my doubts all along, but Caligula himself would find this behavior on the extreme side."

"Down…" My mind had snapped, all right, snapped to a conclusion. "Back down to the cave, Flynn! *Back down to the cave!*"

"That's right, Hudson," said a voice from the doorway, a voice I could not immediately identify because it wasn't coming over a public address system. The ceiling and the four walls lifted up, off the floor, rising back up into Everlasting House, revealing that we were indeed again down in the cave, and again surrounded by the black-robed host.

Luther Ado stood out from the crowd, staring at me menacingly. Flanking him, I couldn't help but notice Peter and a de-gagged Tara, both held firmly in the arms of black-robed guardians.

"See?" I squeaked back over my shoulder. "Elevator room."

Chapter XXV
HEART OF DARKNESS

ADO STRODE TOWARD US, MOVING WITH A SNAKE'S JERKY GRACE-fulness, and for the first time I was treated to a close-up of his features — and surely Luther Ado's forebears had at some point displeased gods from every pantheon, for no one who was born looking like him could possibly turn out as anything other than a villain of surpassing depravity. His eyes attracted one's attention first, primarily because they were entirely black. Either he was afflicted with pupils larger than his irises, or he wore contacts, or the corruption of his soul was manifesting itself physically. His mouth was a line that could have served as a plumb, and his cheekbones came almost to his eyebrows — which arched high up onto his forehead, two thin half-circles that could have been drawn on with a pen. His hair swept down in a widow's peak that tapered just above his nose. And the sight of his skin, so pallid, so dry, so papery, made me long to suggest certain Avon products my mother sold.

But I didn't dare. Some evil you joke with, some evil you don't.

"Miles Hudson," said this creature, and the memories of his pronunciation are enough, even now, to persuade me to give sincere thought to changing my name. "What a fascinating two days you have had, eh?" Ado smiled. His teeth were tiny and had slots between them. "Why do you come to us now and provide the answer we originally sought? Why did you not supply the answer in Humphreys' office, at the allotted juncture? Why make a mockery of our ceremony? Are we marionettes dancing at the end of your strings? Why do you wait" — he leaned his face into me — "until *now?*"

As Ado's face hovered before me, like a cross before a vampire, two opposing frameworks flashed through my consciousness. The first of these was my experience with the amateurish incompetence of this UNKNOWN conspiracy — the result of which was that I hadn't exactly been taking this UNKNOWN conspiracy as seriously as I perhaps ought to have. The second of these was the unmistakable, palpable sheen of wickedness that lay upon Luther Ado...here was a man (if human he was) without a conscience; or at least a superhuman ability to ignore his conscience.

I knew enough of history to be exceptionally frightened of a man like that.

We were in trouble. Big trouble. I had led myself, and, worse, my friends, straight into this mess. Flynn, Gerald, and Peter had trusted me — the fools! — and now the peril in which they found themselves was profound and imminent. The peril in which we *all* found ourselves was profound and imminent — including perhaps even Tara, since she'd been secured by black-robed forearms just as solidly as Peter had been. I tried to gulp again, but my saliva had deserted me. South, it must have headed, in the direction of my bladder.

A moment of truth had been reached. I could either crumple to the floor and beg for mercy or I could see this thing through to the end.

I did not choose the latter course out of any great courage — I chose it out of nothing more than an all-consuming desire not to die. Survival is man's most basic instinct.

I thought quickly. More quickly than I had before or have since. Necessity may be the mother of invention, but confronting a group of black-robed college professors has to count as at least a distant cousin.

I puffed out my chest. "The Western Wing," I said with conviction, "is weak!"

Luther's body tensed.

The next few minutes were as close to an out-of-body experience as I ever hope to have.

I roared, "You have *always* been weak! You make every attempt to imitate the Eastern Wing, instead of being what you are: the Western Wing!"

I stepped back from Ado, and spread out my arms, and addressed the black robes encircling us. I patterned my speech after Ado's, and Mussolini's, and Stalin's, and Pol Pot's.

"The Eastern Wing *has* been testing you…partly in the way you supposed, but your imaginations are dull and limited. The test *was* how you would manage Miles Hudson's intrusion into THE UNKNOWN — but the test was also whether you would discern that Miles Hudson truly was the Eastern emissary, and was playing you all for fools. But *no!*"

I curled my fists with the fake emotion of it all.

"Anything outside your narrow realm of consideration and you are *lost!* Once I failed your test — once I failed to provide Humphreys with that ludicrous handshake" — I rapidly set my hands in eighteen different handshake configurations, to illustrate the absurdity of the whole thing — "the prospect of my being the emissary, which until then was all but a certainty to you, instantly became unthinkable."

I spun in a slow circle.

"The Eastern Wing's test was unfair, you say? Is that what I hear you say? If so you are still in the thrall of your weakness! Instead of bemoaning your bad fortune, you must admit your failure — you must *learn* from your failure! Let your failure loosen the bonds of your imaginations!"

I paused to allow this high note to echo throughout the cavern. I was beginning to understand the attraction of mass public-speaking. Mussolini wasn't really after fascism, Stalin wasn't really after communism, Pol Pot wasn't really after genocide...they just enjoyed working the crowds.

I continued:

"Another example of your provincialism is Tara Fury. She comes from the East, she tells you! Miles Hudson is not the emissary, she tells you! Justin Time is the emissary, she tells you!"

Tara's eyes grew large as Little Orphan Annie's. I shook my head theatrically. "And you people *fell* for it!"

One thousand or so black hoods bowed in shame.

One, however, did not.

Luther Ado's stare was that of Robert Frost coming to a fork in the road...would he believe me or would he not? To believe me meant conceding his blunders and abrogating his authority — to disbelieve me meant jeopardizing his accord with the Eastern Wing. The question was, how hungry was Luther Ado for rapprochement? The internal battle between the two options must have raged furiously, but his face never changed, not a molecule. Stolid, impassive, intimidating — his visage would have been right at home on Easter Island.

He paced toward me, across the dis-walled, dis-ceilinged floor of Dr. Humphreys' library. When he spoke it was with a new and disarming gentility.

"THE UNKNOWN is well-schooled in division. In discord. Schisms have ever endangered that unity without which we are foredoomed to ruin. It began with Barbara Blanding — fratricide! What sort of solution is that? And the sad woman reaped what she had sown! Overthrown and murdered by her own acolytes! And then her sins repeated in the next generation, by William and Davis Cranston! To this day their sins divides us — we stand here today the creations of that rift between brother and sister, brother and brother!"

Ado turned and contemplated Peter, compassion in his eyes. It was easy to forget that Ado had been speaking of Peter's father and uncle. "We have lost so much. We have lost too much!"

He put his hand on Peter's shoulder, commiserating. "So much...too much!"

He addressed the hushed cavern and raised his hands. "It is time — it is high time! — we were *one* again!"

The black robes let out an ear-shattering cheer.

Luther Ado walked over and embraced me the way Stanley must have embraced Dr. Livingstone.

I presume.

CHAPTER XXVI
PANTS ON FIRE

WE WERE LED THROUGH THE DOOR THAT HAD BEEN SO INCONVEN-
iently closed off during our previous visit, into a much
smaller adjoining cavern. Its roof, liberally stalactited, was
visible above, though still at a good elevation. This was Luther's office, evidently, replete with beeping and blinking
electronic paraphernalia — banks of phones and fax ma-
chines, at least a dozen television screens, and at least two
dozen more computer screens with data cycling across them
faster than the eye could follow.

Luther, sitting at a keyboard console, motioned to the
black robes holding Peter and Tara. The robes let go their cap-
tives' arms, then melted silently into the shadows.

Tara said, as if it were indisputable fact, "You made the
wrong choice, Luther."

Engrossed in his typing, Ado paid her little heed. I took
advantage of the lull to gather my wits, with which my performance as the Eastern emissary had played a game of 52-
pick up. I shall never quite understand where I found the
thespianical skill to pull that one off, but I was too concerned
with continuing to pull it off to present myself the Tony
Award which, in retrospect, I so richly deserved.

Luther's fingers rap-rap-rapped on the keys. He almost
seemed to have forgotten that anyone else was in the room.

He said, airily, as if he were typing the words as he spoke them, "We embark on an enterprise of such magnitude…"

His words hung in the air. No one dared utter a sound. I snuck a glance toward Flynn, but he was preoccupied with the room's technology. Once upon a times, Flynn had been a ham radio operator, a computer programmer, a cable installer, a telephone repairman, etc., so he did have a passing acquaintance with modern machinery.

Luther Ado poked a final key with his middle finger and leaned back in his chair. He eyed each of the room's television monitors in turn. From my angle I couldn't tell what was on those monitors, but Luther appeared to be pleased by what he saw.

"We shall achieve the impossible," he said. "We shall reconcile the irreconcilable. The path is planned! The scheme is set! The journey lies before us!"

Out of the corner of my eye I saw Gerald's eyes roll toward me, and the message they relayed was, *If life is a poker game, this man is not playing with half a deck. He is playing with Uno cards.*

"What *is* your scheme, Luther?" asked Tara. "Your harebrainwashed bevy of Grim Reapers couldn't change a flat tire, from what I've seen."

Luther stood in a quick motion, his dark eyes flashing. "They're going to remake the world," he hissed.* He approached Tara with more of a slide than a walk, the way a fakir approaches a cobra…Tara's face took on the dull glaze of the enchanted, and I had the crazy thought that Ado might possess a Shadow-y talent for usurping others' minds.

---

* Don't ask me how a person can hiss a sentence with no sibilants, but that's what he did.

"*Who are you?*" said his voice to her, though his lips did not move.

"She's an intruder," I blurted out anxiously.

"I am asking *her*," Ado said mildly. "If she is not from the Eastern Wing, where *is* she from?"

His head leaned close to hers, their profiles silhouetted against the flickering screens behind them. "Whence came you?" he ventriloquisted.

Her mouth opened and she spoke too openly, too carefreely, for her words to have been those of the Tara Fury I had come to know — this was the *true* Tara Fury talking, this was Tara Fury in her memoirs published after her death, when she had nothing to fear and nothing to lose:

"I am from the Eastern Wing. I was born in Atlanta, the daughter of Ashley Cranston and Richard Fury. My father died just after I was born, and my mother raised me on her own — or so she assumed. Her family recruited me into THE UNKNOWN when I was ten years old. She never knew. She still doesn't know. I went to college and graduate school, proved my worth — in due time I was assigned to be an assistant to Justin Time, one of the Eastern Wing's leading lights. When he was assigned to be the emissary to the Western Wing, I was assigned to accompany him as backup and support."

Ado's head jerked back. Tara's face regained its color, and she blinked rapidly. Her entire body reflexively snapped away from Ado when she realized how near he was. Into her eyes came the dawning realization of what had just occurred — what she had just said.

Ado's head now swiveled toward me. His face flickered in the light. His eyes were slits. "They do not usually lie when under my spell, Miles. Some few have...but they are rare indeed. She is either telling the truth, or she is a liar of uncommon caliber."

My brain scrambled for a rebuttal. It latched onto the first thing it could think of. Once again, what an unfortunate shame that there wasn't a studio audience present to appreciate the heights I reached that morning.

"Wouldn't you," I said, licking my lips to grease the whopper passing through them, "wouldn't you *expect* Jacques Le Monde to be a liar of uncommon caliber?"

*   *   *

Flynn's entire face fell in on itself. Gerald's head drooped in disbelief, a reaction he'd had much opportunity to practice of late. Tara's eyebrows did a slow pirouette. She looked at me with what I took to be a newfound admiration — here, indeed, she must have been thinking, was a liar of uncommon caliber.

"Who's Jacques Le Monde?" asked Peter.

Ado retreated from Tara. "He is an agent of the French Sûreté. A very famous agent. A very *male* agent."

"Until a few short months ago," I said, my creative juices percolating even as my common sense evaporated. "At which time his frustration with his inability to penetrate THE UNKNOWN became so acute that he decided to take truly drastic measures — and what more perfect cover is there than being female when the world knows you as a male?"

I was commanding the room again, and was reminded of my experience with The Bruce Washington Show. I smiled an omniscient smile at Tara. "I'll say this for you, Le Monde — you're dedicated. Not many would give up their manhood for their career."

Peter's jaw was quivering. He was on the verge of declaring, "What are you talking about, moron, that's my niece!

I've known her since she was born! And she was born with *girl parts!*"

But Flynn's collapsed face and Gerald's drooped head were both shaking surreptitiously No, Don't, and my body language was firmly reinforcing this communiqué. Eight or ten seconds lingered like radioactivity as Peter considered, reconsidered, and rereconsidered his position. In the end he clamped his mouth shut, his mandibles meeting with the same sound those inside NORAD hear when the big doors slam together. I trusted it would take a lot more than a nuclear blast to unglue those mandibles, and I would have heaved a tremendous sigh of relief, but at some point in the past few minutes I had apparently stopped breathing.

Ado ogled Tara as if he had x-ray vision. The line of his mouth lengthened. His nostrils flared with suppressed rage. "*Jacques Le Monde*," he whispered. "I see it now...the line of the chin...the intellect hidden just beneath the surface of the eyes...the earlobes, yes!...and the bridge of the nose! It *is* you, Le Monde — I am so foolish not to have seen it before! But my memory is of crushing you in Monte Carlo...you were stupid, stupid! to call *Banco* when you did...oh, Le Monde, Le Monde! How many years you have hounded us? How much time, how many resources, have we wasted to throw you off our scent? And now you are delivered unto us so readily, so easily! Is fate not wonderfully ironic?"

"It certainly is," said Tara, without a trace of distress, with numerous traces of brassy brazenness. I suppose in her place I'd have exhibited the same confidence — she knew, after all, that I was perjuring myself like a Mafia bookkeeper — but it was a tactical mistake on her part, as her brash self-assurance was all the further proof Luther needed that she was in fact the post-operative Jacques Le Monde.

"A fitting punishment!" howled Ado, clenching his fists. "How am I to conceive a fitting punishment for such a nuisance as you at such a time as this? My mind is overflowing, filled with my ultimate triumph in resoldering the Eastern and Western Wings of THE UNKNOWN! I cannot think of aught else! *I cannot think!*"

His glance shot toward me. "I would give the honor to you, who has delivered him to me — but soon your mind will be as full as mine."

There'll still be lots of room left over, I thought.

Ado leapt between Flynn and Gerald, wrapping his fingers around their shoulders. "You! You, who must be the adjutants to the emissary! I give the honor to *you!*"

Flynn stared at him dully, as if he were watching an uninteresting TV program.

Gerald stared at him circumspectly, as if he were watching a love scene on TV with his mother sitting next to him.

"Dwell on it," said Ado. "Do not rush. Take your time. The punishment must be perfect. Our vengeance must be exquisite!"

Gerald swallowed.

Flynn nodded affably. "Sure thing," he said.

CHAPTER XXVII
CHRYSALIS

ADO SNAPPED HIS FINGERS AND THE TWO BLACK ROBES RE-emerged from the shadows.

"Go now," Luther directed. "Leave us to our work."

The black robes took Tara forcibly, while Peter, Gerald, and Flynn followed subserviently — as did I, until Ado held me back, at which point I understood that I was meant to be one of the nouns in the pronoun "us."

When they were gone, Luther loosened the top buttons of his shirt.

"Lord," he said, exhaling, "that's a trial. I don't know how you do it. But you're good, you're *incredibly* good — better than I'll ever be, that's for sure."

He looked at me then and smiled — the transformation that had come over him was extraordinary. His expression was...*warm*.

"Sorry to put you through all that, but you know how it is. Gotta put on a show for the masses. Mind-reading, shmind-reading — you do a little sideshow-level hypnosis and they lap it up like kittens at a milk bowl."

He reached up to his left eye. When his hand came down, it held a black-tinted contact lens. The eye behind it was absolutely normal — pretty, even, being as it was a pleasant shade of green. "Theatrics, theatrics, that's all they ever talked about in training." He dropped into one chair and pulled a second close to him. "Have a seat," he indicated. "Make yourself comfortable."

I did so, all the while gaping at him. Was this a trick? A ploy to lower my defenses?

"Sorry about this," he said, removing the contact lens from the other eye, which, as it turned out, was not so pleasant to look at. Mottled, gray, swollen, it made a poor partner to its leftward counterpart. "Had an accident a few months ago," he said apologetically. "It's still healing."

"Yes, we — er — we heard about that," I said, in an attempt to perpetuate the Myth Of The Omniscient Eastern Emissary — a wildly successful attempt, for if Jesus Christ had ridden into the room on the back of a unicorn, I don't think Luther would have regarded him with a more unalloyed veneration than he did me, at that moment. His eyes, the good and the bad, were lit like stars, and he all but hugged himself with contented glee.

"So *you're* the Eastern emissary after all," he said. "Talk about a shocker! And Tara Fury is *Jacques Le Monde?* I'd never have figured that out in a million years!" Now he laughed out loud, a young laugh, a child's laugh. "Boy, are you guys on the ball in the East! You're absolutely right, by the way, about our always trying to imitate you, instead of being ourselves. And that's mostly my fault, I have to admit." He smiled, friendly as a door-to-door salesman. "But like I say, you guys are so *on the ball!* Is it any wonder we try to copy you?"

"I understand," I said, though I did not.

"Just my luck to be born in Denver," he joked. "Stuck with the Western Wing!"

I laughed along with him. My hypocrisy was Pharasaical.

"But, really," Luther said, "we haven't done *so* terribly bad, have we? We've built up an infrastructure, we've got a good group of people, nobody's the wiser — no, sir, I don't think we have too much to bow our heads over."

I remembered the advice of my high school drama teacher. *Never* break character.

"You've constructed a unique organization," I said, "but its uniqueness is what you must learn to take advantage of. Maximize your intrinsic potential. Play to your strengths, Luther."

"Oh, please," he laughed, "don't call me that! It's Bruce."

Nature, commonly, has a humane policy as regards revelations that astonish or stupefact us — she spreads them out over the course of our lifetimes. We don't, for instance, discover one day that we are adopted and the next day that we've been fired and the day after that that we've won the Lotto. But Nature had, from the look of things, taken an extended vacation without leaving her secretary a number where she might be reached, and so the revelations were coming fastly and furiously. There weren't this many surprises in a whole case of Cracker Jacks.

For Luther Ado was none other than my student, the conspiracy buff, Bruce Washington.

*   *   *

When wearing stomach padding and a false beard and going without a shower for three days, that is. The man was a chameleon inhabiting, at current count, three different and distinct personae as alike one another as three planets taken at random. Schizophrenic? Possibly. Psychotic? Certainly. Damned likable? Yes, consarn it — at least, this latest personality, Bruce Without The Makeup, was as likable as could be.

The kind of guy you hoped your sister would meet and marry, but never did.

Bruce leaned close to me, a wicked (this adjective here using its playful, as opposed to its cruel, definition; I empathize with your bewilderment) grin splashing onto his face. "Miles—" The grin disappeared, replaced by an expression of utmost concern. "It is okay if I call you Miles?"

"Sure," I said benevolently.

The grin reappeared. "Miles — that's *exactly* what I'm up to."

"Oh?" said I, as if I already knew the answer to my own question, but asked it out of politeness anyway. "What *exactly* are you up to?"

"Playing to our strengths! My plan is foolproof, it's perfect, it's a stroke of genius!" He blushed. He actually blushed. "If," he added, "you'll pardon the immodesty."

At this point I'd have pardoned Sirhan Sirhan if Luther/Bruce had asked me to, so taken was I with his new personality.

I said, "Confidence is commendable. Confidence is what you've lacked. But you don't want to go overboard. Confidence must be tempered by reality."

"Let's see how *this* reality strikes you," retorted Bruce. "The town of Constant...*erased*."

"You'd need a very big pencil," was my reply.

Bruce laughed. He laughed so hard he fell out of his chair.

I was beginning to discern the outlines of the man's underlying psychology. He suffered from a definite lack of self-esteem — he was far too eager to please. In his childhood he had probably lacked a father figure; a strong figure of authority. Now he lampreyed onto any strong figure of authority that came down the pike, including a blatant forgery like me.

Bruce crawled back into his chair. *"That's* why I became Bruce Washington, Miles. Just to sit in on one of your classes and enjoy that Dr. Miles Hudson wit."

"Ah," I said, as if this wasn't the first time a participant in one of my classes had put "wit" and "Dr. Miles Hudson" next to each other in the same sentence.

"Hey, wasn't that Tomkinson a hoot? The Bible! *Japanese!"*

With this he slid out of his chair again, and did not return for some minutes.

"How you kept from cracking up I do not know!"

"Bruce, I'm curious about your plan. Explain to me the particulars. *Erase* Constant?"

"Yes!"

"The town?"

"Yes!"

"The *entire* town?"

"Yes!"

"How?"

"Bombs."

"Bombs?"

"Yes, bombs."

"Bombs."

"Uh-huh."

"How many bombs?"

"Quite a few. You'd be surprised how many it takes. Whoever said it's easier to destroy than to create never tried to blow up a whole town!"

The man was charming and likable, but I'd allowed myself to forget that he was nonetheless a psychopath. He'd fooled me for a while with his Falstaffian personality, but I was no longer the immature and susceptible Henry of *Henry IV*. I was now the experienced, wiser *Henry V*.

"How many is quite a few?" I asked. "And where did you come by so many bombs? And precisely what good will come of blowing up Constant?"

"Quite a few is 50," answered Bruce. "And we didn't 'come by' them — this'll show you we've got some initiative — we *made* them! Yep, made 'em ourselves — homemade dynamite! Yuri was a load of help, believe you me. Couldn't have done it without him."

"Yuri....*Zelikov?*" I asked, as if there were Yuri Smiths and Yuri Joneses roaming around Constant.

"Yeah," said Bruce. "Guy's aces. Just the best."

"Hmm," I said, my voice catching a little.

"As for your final question...well..." A mischievous glint shot out from the center of his left eye. "We're moving."

He did not clarify, he merely stared at me as if expecting a small biscuit. At length I said, "Oh, are you?"

"Yeah!" he yelped. "We're movin' to Frisco!"

Again he did not clarify, and again he stared. At length I said, "Oh, you are?"

"Yeah! Got the new buildings all ready, got our stuff all packed, we're headin' on out! San Francisco, here we come!"

I thought, as I so often had during this affair, that I understood now.

"You're blowing up Constant to remove all traces of your presence."

He put his finger along the right side of his nose. "You got it. But that's not the only reason. It's not even the main reason, to tell the truth." He nodded his head as if even he couldn't accept the sheer breathtaking magnificence of the scheme he'd imagined. "We're doing something *spectacular* here. Something *memorable*. Something" — the rest of his face apologized profusely for this comment even as his mouth produced it — "the Eastern Wing has never done."

I thought, *Gee, I wonder why.*

I sat silent momentarily, pretending to ponder in silence the sheer breathtaking magnificence of his scheme — which I was in fact doing, if one replaces the word "magnificence" with "daftness." Luther watched me like a Little Leaguer looking over at his dad after getting his first hit.

I asked, "Where are the bombs planted?"

Luther chuckled to himself. "That's the beauty part. It's ingenious!"

Oh, so you're using gophers, I thought.

"We got Bob Twilley* to show us stress points, load-bearing walls, all that good stuff. The place'll collapse in on itself like a door to another universe!"

"But where, Bruce? *Where* are the bombs?"

"I'll show you in a second. But what do you think? Is this plan brilliant or is this plan brilliant?"

The only answer to that question being *No!*, I decided to ignore it. "What timeframe are you working with? When do the bombs go off?"

He replied, "Tomorrow at noon."

"Oh." My voice cracked like a 13-year old boy's. "Really?"

---

* Constant College's Professor of Structural Engineering, the one member of the faculty with whom I didn't get along — but only because Bob Twilley didn't get along with anyone. He was known to conduct arguments even with himself, many of which he lost.

Chapter XXVIII
HEARTBREAK

BRUCE LED ME ALONG A DAMP, SHADOWY PASSAGEWAY. LIGHT seeped down around us from dilapidated lamps hanging on rusty chains high above. We walked — him without caution, me with much — on moss-coated slats of wood covering the uneven stone floor. Fat drops of water pelted us from the ceiling, drops with, the ceiling being a distance away, quite a head of steam on them. I held up my hand as a makeshift umbrella, but the drops were too large, too quick, and too numerous to avoid — the inside of a sinking submarine would have been less soggy. Five minutes into the trip my clothes were soaked.

But what was worse — a great deal worse — was the growing stench. We were drawing closer to the sewers with every step, and every breath I took I held a little longer. I was respirating at the rate of an elephant by the time Bruce stopped and turned to me and said, "Here we are."

He stood at a railing, beyond which and parallel to which ran a river. Hard to tell in the dimness, but it appeared to be a dozen or so feet deep, flowing at a slow and leisurely pace. In both directions it disappeared out of view into branching caves. To our left, stacked high, were at least fifty cardboard boxes, all of which had *California Hobby Supplies, Inc., San Diego, CA* stenciled on their sides.

"You must have figured it out by now!" said Bruce happily. "It must be plain as the nose on your face!"

He was incorrect, for while his plan was plain, the nose on my face was not, in this light.

"Float the bombs under their targets," I said. "Constant *will* collapse…right into the ground."

"I knew you'd approve!" clucked Bruce. "Yuri's an avid R.C.'er, too."[*]

"Yes…I've seen him at the stadium with his planes…"

"He also does boats! We'll drive 'em from here, detonate 'em all at the same time…*kaboom!* Now *that's* theatrics!"

I fought to catch my breath, not just from the audacity of his now-revealed plan, but also from the throat-constricting reek of the Constant sewer system.

"Bruce, I…applaud…your creativity. But as the Eastern emissary I feel compelled to make it known that the complete destruction of THE UNKNOWN's premier facility this side of the Mississippi is not what might be called a thrilling prospect for we in the Eastern Wing."

Bruce had an answer for this.

"But we're upgrading! Frisco's a *much* better platform for our types of operations, and the recruiting — well, don't even start with me on the recruiting. You ever tried to convince a Nobel laureate to teach at a 1500-student college? It's like pulling teeth, and once or twice that's what it's come to. I understand your concerns, Miles, but trust me — the Western Wing is on the upswing. That's our new motto. D'you like it? *The Western Wing — on the upswing!*"

---

[*] R.C.: radio-controlled. R.C.'er: a person who enjoys pouring hundreds of dollars into a project that, with one wrong jerk of a thumb on a control stick, flies right into the side of a cliff, or drives right off the side of a cliff, or sails right over a waterfall on the side of a cliff. If you are an R.C.'er, a cliffside will inevitably enter your life.

"It's…" I said.

"Please, trust me, Miles," implored Bruce. "We know what we're doing. We're young and we're inexperienced and, yes, darn it, we're probably overenthusiastic, but you can't question our dedication and our resolve." He was frighteningly serious, gawking at me through puppy-dog eyes. He seized me by the shoulders. "Miles, have faith — you have nothing to fear when it comes to our ability to get the job done."

He was correct, at least, about that, although not in the manner he meant. With the Western Wing's track record, the bombs would probably float far into the Pacific before exploding harmlessly.

But I couldn't take the chance that Bruce/Luther and his minions would find a way to screw this up — even the most incompetent of conspiracies gets something right sometime, and the consequences of their getting this one right were dire beyond description. Even if the odds of THE UNKNOWN's turning my current hometown into a sinkhole were $\infty : 1$ against, I had to do everything within my power to make those odds $\infty + 1 : 1$.

"Are the bombs armed?" I asked.

"Not yet," said Bruce. "Too dangerous."

"That's done by remote control, as well?"

"Nope. By hand. Detonated by remote, though."

He tore open the flaps of one of the cardboard boxes and lifted from it a miniature fishing trawler. The *Daisy May or May Not*, out of Baton Rouge, from the red-painted markings on her stern.

"Isn't that neat?" said Bruce. "They're individualized. Special feature the hobby company offers. Costs a little more, but it's worth it. Rather be blown up by the *Daisy May Or*

May Not than some nameless radio-controlled speedboat, wouldn't you?" He slapped me on the back.

"Rather not be blown up at all," I joked weakly.

"Ha!" said he.

"And," said I, taking the trawler into my hands, "they're armed how?"

"Right here," he said, before he could stop the chuckling and begin the wondering why I should want to know such a thing. He pointed at the trawler's intricately detailed deck, where a suavely-dressed miniature captain in sweater and pleated pants entertained a scantily-clad young lady in bikini and wide-brimmed sun hat. A pitcher of margaritas sat on a nearby table. I did not stop to wonder why a man would choose as his location for the romancing of a young lady the deck of a fishing boat.

"You turn the capstan one revolution to the left," said Bruce. "You hear a beep and she's all set."

He brought out from his shirt pocket a credit card-sized metal box. "This is the detonator. One little button's all it takes."

"And what if," I continued, "they all went off in the same location — one large explosion instead of fifty smaller ones."

"That's what you'd get," said Bruce. "One large explosion instead of fifty smaller ones."

"But the level of destruction, is what I'm asking. How much damage would be done to Constant if every one of these were set off right here, underground?"

Bruce looked puzzled. "I dunno...we never studied the stress points in this area. There's nothing aboveground but fields, wide-open space. Probably no damage at all, 'cept folks would wonder where the big bowl in the earth came from."

"The cave? Everlasting House?"

"Ummmmmmm — again, I dunno. We sure as heck never studied the stress points for them, either. We're...oh...two or three kilometers from Everlasting House. Might seem like a small earthquake to them, or it might seem like Krakatoa to them." He shrugged. "I'm sorry to be vague, Miles, but I can't give you a definitive answer. My mom always said, *Unless you turned into God while I wasn't looking, don't be a know-it-all.*"

Bruce/Luther was still the most well-adjusted and amiable psychotic I'd ever crossed paths with, but he had, irritatingly, and unknowingly, thrown a wrench into my newly-formed course of action, a solution that had popped into my brain that fit the circumstances like the shoe fit Cinderella. The solution was: knock Bruce unconscious, arm a single bomb, carry Bruce to a safe distance, and then detonate the bomb, obliterating the entire stockpile.

The wrench in this solution was, What was a safe distance? I could only go as far as the cave without being discovered, and if the cave wasn't far enough away to escape the explosion unscathed, then — our goose was cooked.

Literally.

It's possible that most other red-blooded American would have thought nothing of being blown into dust, if doing so would prevent the loss of thousands of other lives — but *this* red-blooded American had the sudden and immediate thought that he should change his citizenship.

Still, I had not, as I told Jacques Le Monde without his hearing me, come this far only to give up. THE UNKNOWN had to be stopped. If I had to die to stop it — so be it.[*]

---

[*] I actually did think this, at that moment: *If I have to die to stop THE UN-KNOWN — so be it.* I don't present this self-glorificationally, but rather as

For when, I reasoned, would an opportunity like this come around again? I was alone — alone! — with the leader of the pack, the deviser of the devious design, the man without whom the Western Wing would collapse like Constant tomorrow at noon.

And he was unarmed!   Defenseless!   Suspicionless! Clueless!

How could I possibly let such a situation go by and still call myself a conspiracy-fighter?

I couldn't.

So I punched him.

But he scarcely noticed, so I clapped the boat across the side of his head.

He fell to the wooden floor in slow motion, his eyes staring at me all the way down — his one bright and lively eye, his one dull and damaged eye, both now shocked and horrified at this betrayal. Their light slowly faded, ebbing into nothingness…testifying to a heartbreak Juliet, King Priam, and Neville Chamberlain all put together never knew.

---

an instance of my emerging understanding that given the proper impetus, a person really will say (or think) a sentence like *If I have to die to stop* THE UNKNOWN — *so be it.*

CHAPTER XXIX
THE ENDS JUSTIFIES

THE QUESTION "WHAT SHALL I DO WITH THE BODY?" WAS NOT one that, even in the most far-flung of my meandering day-dreams, I had ever envisioned having to ask myself. (Insofar as one can envision audio.) But there I was, one hundred and sixty pounds of dead weight at my feet and the splintered remains of a bayou trawler in my right hand, with nary a word of decent explanation as to how either came to be.

A lesson came to mind: *Think before you act.*

But I did think! I shot back.

You thought wrong, came the lesson.

Where were you a second ago? I asked, outraged.

Lessons follow mistakes. They don't precede them.

I'd make the same mistake again, if you were standing here instead of Luther!

Oh, look at the big talker, said the lesson.

Now an idea came to mind.

That just might work, said the lesson.

Oh, I've given it enough thought, have I? I replied sarcastically.

Not by half. But like the Western Wing, you'd probably only screw it up if you did.

You're not much of a lesson, are you? Think before you act — don't *think before you act. If I were you I'd stop calling myself a lesson and start calling myself a situational ethic.*

The lesson answered with a tremendous headache.

*   *   *

"Luther Ado," I said to the pair of black robes who'd been guarding Flynn, Gerald, Peter, and Tara, "has taken the secret passageway up to the surface. He had some business at the hardware store."

I felt like Jacob trying to fool Isaac.

The black robe on the left turned to the black robe on the right and, from what I could see of his mouth, grinned, and, from what I could see of his arm, nudged his companion in the stomach. "Him and that hardware," he said.

His companion snorted. "Yeah."

They both returned their attention to me.

And said no more — leaving me to scythe my way through the several dozen different possible meanings of their brief dialogue. None of which meanings, at first glance from my mind's eye, gave the appearance of being the sort of place my mind's eye would care to linger.

I chose rather to rejoice that these two Isaacs were falling for my goatskins. "His wishes," I said, full of that manic confidence that swells up in a man's breast when one of his lies is believed, "were for me to take the prisoner Le Monde to the underground dock. We will place her — him — at the center of the blast."

The two guards glanced at one another.

"Wow," said the one on the right. "That is one *great* idea. This was Mr. Ado's idea? You said it was *his* wish, but you don't take orders from him, you're the Eastern emissary. You *way* outrank him."

"Yeah," said the one on the left. "I'll bet it was *your* idea, huh?"

They gawped at me expectantly.

I lowered my eyes. "It was a joint effort," I said, not without modesty.

The one on the left shook his head in admiration. "What I wouldn't give to have been born in Pittsburgh, or Bangor, or Charleston." He lifted his gaze to the ceiling. "The Eastern Wing," he whispered. "The Eastern Wing..."

"Aw, chin up," said the one on the right, nudging his partner with his elbow once again. "'Least we got to meet the Eastern emissary in person."

This brought a stifled gurgle from Tara.

"Bring Le Monde to me," I said. "And my assistants, as well."

"Yes, *sir!*" said them both in unison, giving me a bizarre signal with their arms that I took to be the Western Wing's version of a salute. It was performed so quickly, and took me so by surprise, that I couldn't tell what it entailed, exactly — but in those heavy robes, they could have been doing the merengue and all I'd have seen was a slight undulation about the hips.

The two guards scurried to their task. I folded my arms together and ruminated once again that, whatever the outcome of the next few minutes and hours, my life as I'd known it was over. I could never be plain old Miles Hudson, Ph.D., mild-mannered professor of history, again. If I succeeded in stopping THE UNKNOWN in Constant, I would forever be looking over my shoulder for their inevitable retaliation. If I did not succeed, my life would be *over*, period, regardless of how I'd known it.

I'll just have to succeed, then, I said to myself. But what would my life look like, post-success? Would I go into hiding? Would I become a Bruce Washington clone, spreading the gospel of the dangers of THE UNKNOWN to an unknowing, uncaring world? Would I take the fight to THE UNKNOWN in other parts of the world? Who did I think I was, Zorro?

"Old hoss!"

The sound of Flynn's voice brought me back to the present. I blinked to focus my eyes. Flynn approached, followed by Peter and Gerald, and by the two guards, each of whom held one of Tara's arms.

"Thank heavens you're all right!" said Flynn, grasping my hand, displaying a degree of friendship and camaraderie that just wouldn't do between the Eastern emissary and his assistant.

I refused his hand and hoped he'd understand. And play along. "I see in your short time among them the Westerners have already begun to corrupt you, Mr. Flynn. Such blatant disregard for protocol will *not* be tolerated, is that clear?"

Although I spoke these words in a manner and volume befitting a Niagara tour guide warning a child to get down off that railing, my right eyelid was doing a jig, attempting to wink without winking. Flynn's naturally cheery disposition initially recoiled at my rebuke, but then he caught on.

"I beg your humble pardon," he said, bowing on one knee and prostrating himself before me. "Punish me as you see fit. I live but to serve."

When Flynn caught on, he *caught on*. The two guards gaped at me as if they were ten years old and I was Willy Wonka.

"You'll not be needed any longer—" I said to them, and they were gone before the final syllable had left my lips.

"Well played," sneered Tara. "You're quite the actress."

"Do you want to be gagged again?" I said by way of riposte.

She quieted.

"Now then," I said, ringing in the others, "here's where we stand."

I proceeded to outline the situation for them, and summarized my plan of attack. The guards had unwittingly confirmed that a secret passageway to the surface *did* exist — which had been a wild guess on my part (or, more correctly, a guess founded on my sketchy knowledge of gothic romances). My Pollyanna plan would work after all — set the bomb, make our way to the surface and a safe distance, detonate the bomb, destroy Ado's stockpile.

As Ado had boasted of his plan: ingenious.

"Blow them *all* up?" protested Gerald. "Did you get a doctorate in demolitions while I wasn't looking, Dr. Hudson? You can't predict the consequences of a blast like that! You don't even know how much TNT he's got!"

"He does have a point, Miles," said Peter. "If it's enough to demolish Constant, who can say what effect it'll have? It could start a chain reaction—"

"An earthquake!" blurted Gerald.

"Or an underground fire," said Peter.

"I'm open to suggestions," I said testily. "How else do we get rid of that much dynamite? We can't carry it out with us."

Gerald spoke up again. "The dynamite is in the boats, you say?"

"Yes."

His face brightened. "We start the boats on their ways and smash the detonator. The boats will run until they're out of gas, and then they'll be lost forever. Without the detonator they can't be detonated!"

"And what if," I said, "some child finds one of those boats washed up on the beach somewhere? 'Hey, mommy, look what I found!' *KABLAM!*"

Peter gave me a pained look. "That's rather cruel, Miles."

"I'm not the one who's suggesting it!"

"I never suggested blowing up a child, either," said Gerald, as if some part of him hadn't discounted the possibility.

Flynn, who had been standing back in the shadows, now stepped into the light. His face was set with deeply etched lines of determination, and in his eyes burned a resolve unlike any I'd seen before.

"THE UNKNOWN has to be *destroyed*," he said. "We've had the remarkable good fortune of finding two things in proximity: the Western Wing and a tremendous heap of trinitrotoluene. Why not kill two birds with one stone?"

Tara's eyes fired with diabolical admiration. *She is pure evil*, I thought in passing. *She doesn't care that her comrades will be incinerated, she only cares that it's a cunning stratagem.*

Three mouths opened simultaneously to debate Flynn's proposal, but mine was the quickest. "Your decimal points are off, Flynn. We wouldn't be killing two birds. We'd be killing two or three hundred human beings. And it wouldn't be with one stone — it'd be with several dozen toy boats, all of which are sitting in boxes about a mile away. We don't have time to cart them all back here. And even if we did have time, I'm not prepared to commit murder. I *know* most of those people. Yes, they're involved in a world-wide conspiracy, and yes, they intend to blow up a small town, and yes, they're amoral villains — but I will not stoop to their level in order to stop them."

I stood before them like a portcullis. "We're running out of time and we're running out of options. We don't have the luxury of discussing this in the General Assembly."

Flynn, much abashed, lifted his eyes sheepishly. "Gosh, old goat…it was just a thought."

"Yeah, you don't have to bite his head off," added Gerald.

"And I thought *I* was wound up tight," snorted Peter.

"Oh, what a bunch of hypocrites!" groaned Tara. "How many times have you *lied* in the past forty-eight hours, Hudson? That wasn't stooping to our level? You sucker-punched Luther! *That* wasn't stooping to our level?"

The questions hung in the air like a menacing mobile. The others looked to me for some reply, some response, some defense.

I chose, alternately, to retreat. "Let's get going," I said, and we did.

CHAPTER XXX
SIGNALS

UPON RETURNING TO THE ALCOVE WHICH HOUSED THE BOMBS, THE alcove where I'd "sucker-punched" Bruce/Luther (a comment that wounded me deeply, as in my experience the truth always does), two items of note caught my attention straight away.

The first of these was that Bruce was awakening, slowly, groggily, holding his hand to his temple and shaking his head.

The second of these was that the alcove no longer housed the bombs — every last one of the boxes stood opened and empty.

I stopped short, a quizzical expression plastered on my face. Bruce was just now reviving, so he couldn't have moved the boats. I'd been gone for half an hour at the most, in any case — hardly time enough for one person to pry open four dozen boxes and unload their cargo.

"Well, this is just great," I said to myself.

"What was that, old tom?"

"Nothing, Flynn."

"I thought perhaps you were remarking on the distinctive lack within this chamber of explosive-laden radio-controlled boats."

"They *were* here. They were in these boxes."

"Are you sure of what you saw, Dr. Hudson? It's not uncommon to suffer hallucinations under high-stress conditions—"

"Gerald, I did not hallucinate the boats."

"This stench would drive any man to see things," said Peter, his face a rictus of discomfiture. "I'm seeing myself, as an example, taking a week-long bath."

Bruce muttered a moan. "Miles," he said, pained and perplexed, "Miles, what's going on?"

"Cuff him," I instructed Gerald.

If you should ever seek proof that life is *never* easy, *always* complicated, consider this: I could not watch Gerald handcuff this man — who was on the verge of remorselessly extinguishing thousands of innocent lives — without feeling wretchedly guilty. The expression he cast my way was so pathetic, so pitiful...he had trusted me completely, and I had betrayed him.

How was I any better than Tara, or Justin Time, or Ado himself? All of us pretending to be someone we weren't.

Tara, witnessing this maudlin scene, rolled her eyes yet again. "Oy vey!" she called to the ceiling. "Ado, the word 'boob' was invented for you — specially invented, by the people at the Oxford English Dictionary, just for you. Hudson was lying to you all along! If you'd spared half a second to slip your brain into gear and *think*, you'd have realized just how full of holes his story was! An anvil would have a better chance of staying afloat! —*Mmmmffff!*"

Flynn had whipped out the rag and stuffed it in.

"Thanks, Flynn," I said tiredly. "Bruce — Luther — whoever you are — I apologize for lying to you. Which is laughable, because I shouldn't feel bad for lying to a world-class whack job like you, but nonetheless it's true. You may be one of the nicest, sweetest people I've ever met, but you're still going to prison for the rest of your life."

Tara fell over laughing.

"*She* was telling the truth," whispered Bruce. "Justin Time *was* the emissary..." He looked at me with a sudden sharpness in his eyes. "You *lied* to me, Miles?"

"Where'd the boats go, Bruce?" I asked, blithely ignoring his question.

"The boats?" His eyes narrowed as he looked around for the first time and saw the empty boxes. He tried to stand, but couldn't find his balance with his hands cuffed. Gerald lifted him to his feet. "They're gone!" Bruce wailed. "Where'd they go? Miles, what did you do with the boats? The bombs!"

"Nothing," I replied. "What did *you* do with the boats?"

"Nothing," he replied, frowning. "So where'd they go?"

"I wasn't gone long enough for anything other than a work crew of 100 to finish unpacking all those boxes," I said. "In the absence of any other evidence of a work crew of 100, I'm stumped as to how the job got done."

"But it *did* get done," inserted Peter. "Someone moved them."

Gerald, however, still had his doubts as to my ocular veracity. "Can you say for sure those boxes were full, Dr. Hudson?"

"Bruce opened one," I began—

"Who's Bruce?"

"I mean Luther. Luther opened one of the boxes and took out a radio-controlled boat and he said that you armed the bombs by turning the capstan one revolution to the left. Is that not right, Bruce?"

Bruce turned his nose up and his face to the side.

"He's not agreeing with you, Dr. Hudson."

"He's the *bad guy*, Gerald! And he's in handcuffs! Of course he's not going to be cooperative!"

"Well," huffed Gerald, "if you're sure those boxes were full—"

"I'm sure. I may have begun to doubt that the sky is blue, and I may have begun to doubt that the earth is round, but I am *sure* that those boxes were full."

"Miles," said Bruce, and it seemed as if he genuinely meant it, "I regret this very much. I wish you'd left me some other choice, but — gosh, I'm sorry."

I stared at him, oblivious as to what he was talking about.

"Sorry for what, Ado?" demanded Flynn. "You regret what very much?"

"This," said Bruce.

His lower and upper jaws came together with a sudden snap.

Flynn snorted. "Rather a trivial thing to regret, Ado. I grind my teeth when I sleep, but I don't feel compelled to say an Ave Maria each morning—"

A choking gasp, followed by Tara's rasping laughter — she'd worked the gag out of her mouth. From her prone position her eyes swept over us with the same derision with which Christ's swept over the moneychangers. "He's signaled his troops!" she cackled. "There's an emergency transmitter in his tooth! Standard issue for THE UNKNOWN!"

I looked to Flynn, who looked to Gerald, who looked to Peter, who looked to me, the expression of panic growing as it forwarded from face to face around the room. When it returned to me, I readied my throat for a good screech, a good cat-with-a-paw-stepped-on screech, but then from down the long passageway started a faraway hum, a sound like an air conditioner whirring to life. This was followed by an insistent rattle that grew steadily in volume.

"What is that, Bruce?"

"It's them, coming to rescue me," he said simply.

"In what, an F-16?"

"In the trucks, I would guess."

"Trucks?"

"Yeah."

"What trucks?"

"The flatbed trucks. How else would we get the boxes down here?"

"You have *trucks*?"

"Yes, Miles."

"Why did we have to walk all that way, if you have *trucks*?"

Bruce lowered his head and looked at the ground. He shuffled his feet shyly. "I...well...I wanted the trip to take a while. I wanted to spend some time with you." His eyes rose to meet mine. "I *like* you, Miles. I always did, from the first day you got here. You're a neat guy. You're *fun*. I was thrilled beyond words when I thought you were the Eastern emissary!" All the light drained from his face. "'Course now that's all gone."

Until that moment I hadn't thought it was possible for a person literally to laugh themselves to death, but I was beginning to fear Tara might do just that. She had reached the point where her laughter was so intense that it went silent, leaving her spasming, convulsing, fighting for breath, her face drenched with tears.

The rattling and the humming were riotous now, echoing about us in the alcove, seeking an escape but finding none. The trucks — if trucks they were, if Bruce was telling the truth — were not far off.

Flynn jumped toward the railing above the river. "We'll swim for it!" he shouted. "Remember Los Angeles, 1984!" (When Greg Louganis had inspired a prepubescent Flynn to take up high-diving, an exercise in Nixonian self-deception that ended scant days later when Carl Lewis inspired him to take up track — luckily before Flynn had found the opportunity to attempt an actual dive.)

"No!" I barked dictatorially. "I have a plan!"

Tara went stone-rigid with laughter. She stood statue-like, not even blinking.

"Maybe swimming for it isn't such a bad idea after all," said Peter, moving toward the railing.

"Current doesn't look *too* bad," Gerald granted.

Headlights appeared down the passageway, inundating the alcove with muddy light. Three trucks, each of which was old enough to have been inspected by Henry Ford himself, squealed to a stop in a rough line abreast. Black robes leapt out from the trucks' cabs, four or five from each, pouring out of the darkness and scampering toward us.

"Halt!" I roared, frightening even myself with my intensity. The black robes pulled up short as if I'd drawn back a curtain and revealed a Gatling gun pointing in their direction. I raised my hand, exposing the little metal box I'd lifted from Bruce while he was out cold. The black robes all sucked in their breaths at once in one great gasp.

"This is the detonator!" I yelled. "I don't know where the bombs have gotten off to, but it's a good bet they're still close enough that if I push this little red button we're all dead!"

The black robes turned from me to Bruce, from Bruce to me, from me to Bruce, as if engrossed in a finals match at Wimbledon. They were each, I reflected, just what a diabolical fiend wanted in a lackey — utterly unable to make a decision on their own.

Bruce made no move, said nothing.

I almost smiled. "Stalemate," I said smugly. I gestured to the black robes. "Move aside, we'll be taking those trucks. Move aside, I said — *now!*"

"Hold on there a moment," rang a familiar voice, as a blur whizzed by me, and I noticed an abrupt deficiency in the palm of my right hand, where seconds earlier the detonator had been resting cozily. I brought down my arm and examined my empty hand, puzzled and possessed of an increasing sense of dismay. Or, more accurately, of doom.

I looked to my right — there, leaning against a stack of the empty boxes, his legs crossed jauntily, casually tossing the detonator into the air and catching it again, was the smarmily smirking figure of Justin Time.

Chapter XXXI
SURPRISE . . .

"I ALWAYS DO SO ENJOY," QUIPPED TIME, "LIVING UP TO MY name."

He threw the detonator into the air a final time, sweeping his arm in an elaborate arc to catch it on its way down, then lightly deposited it into his coat pocket. From which, incidentally, he produced a Walther P-38.

"Stalemate's over," he declared sprightly. "You" — this to the black robes — "grab them."

The black robes, at last free to act without equivocation, jumped forward and seized Gerald and Peter. Flynn made a threatening motion to throw himself over the railing and into the river, but in the end he couldn't and wouldn't, it seemed, leave us to face the music (a dirge, no doubt) alone. He stood down and let the black robes shackle his hands.

Which left me. By coincidence or design, the two black robes who approached me happened to be the same two who'd earlier played Isaacs to my Jacob. They paused for a moment as they reached me, presumably out of respect for the eminence they'd believed me to be, then roughly threw me to the ground and bound my hands together. Each linked an arm under mine and dragged me to my feet.

Time was kneeling over Tara, freeing her from her bonds. He helped her to her feet in a way that left little question that they were, as we would have said in the eighth grade, boyfriend and girlfriend.

Tara reached a finger into her mouth and pulled out a shiny silver object.

"Standard issue for THE UNKNOWN," voiced Time pleasantly. "As soon as she realized you were onto her, Tara bit down on *her* secret molar transmitter."

He fished handcuff keys from his pocket as he walked over to where Ado stood. "I've been following you all along, ever since you left your apartment, Miles — hiding behind trees, skulking in shadows. I even hitched a ride on the back fender of your car!" He turned to me and smiled good-naturedly. "I followed you and Ado here" — whose handcuffs he was now unlocking — "down the passageway, and I saw you deck poor Luther."

He looked at me and clucked his tongue. "Honestly, Miles, is that any way to treat the leader of the Western Wing? A guy who'd grown to admire and respect you, a guy who looked up to you? Your treacherous behavior, frankly, shocks, sickens, and appalls me."

He glared at me for a moment, then fell into his girlish giggle. Tara joined in, though her giggle was distinctly more mannish.

Time removed the handcuffs that bound Ado and held them up for all to see. "There you go, Luth." He looked back at me. "To continue the tale: once you left Ado here out cold, I saw my chance. We've known — the Eastern Wing, that is — about Luther's plan for some time now."

Luther gawked at Time as if he'd just said, "Oh, and I've been having your wife on the weekends."

"Sorry, Luth," said Time, "but there it is. We knew, and we approved. So we stayed out of the way."

Upon hearing that Justin Time — indisputably revealed at last as the emissary of the Eastern Wing — *approved* of his grand design, Luther's mood improved considerably. His grin was that of a child of wealthy parents on Christmas morning.

"Nevertheless," proceeded Time, "the sad fact remains that if *I* hadn't been around, Miles Hudson and his three stooges would have prevented the whole operation from coming off as planned."

If Luther hadn't been manic before, he was well on his way now. His mood darkened like a cloud passing over.

"It was *I* who sailed the bomb-boats," preened Time. "This way there'll be no mistakes. We'll detonate as soon as they've had time to reach their proper positions. I estimate that'll be" — he checked his watch — "fifteen minutes or so. I will take Miss Tara through the secret exit. You, Luther, will take the prisoners and do with them what you will."

He leered and added firmly: "As long as 'what you will' includes killing them."

Peter fainted. Flynn put up a brief struggle against his captors, but his hands were too tightly bound for it to be anything other than token. Gerald glowered at me as if this were all *my* fault. Which, broadly, specifically, and in all ways in-between, it was.

I, ever the thinker, played my final card.

"Are you going to let him do this to you?" I jeered at Bruce. "Let him walk right in and take over? Let *him* grab all the glory? All those months of planning and he steps in at the last moment to be the big hero? You're going to stand for this?"

"Yes, he is," said Time with the same kind of authority with which God said, "Let there be light."

Luther did not look happy, but neither did he look overly anxious to take on the Eastern emissary.

Having trumped my final hand, Time held out his hand to Tara, who laid her petite fingers elegantly in his palm. They sashayed across the alcove to stand before me.

"Ta-ta, Miles," said Time. "Sorry to spoil it all for you at the end, but, *c'est la vie*. Survival of the fittest." He leaned close. "Not that Luther's in any way *fit*," he joked, poking me in the ribs with his elbow. "Up to me to save the day, as usual. But you should be proud, Miles, my man — if not for my meddlesome intrusion, you probably *would* have won. Congratulations, for what it's worth."

"Thanks," I said dolefully.

Time stepped back and Tara stepped forward. "So long, Miles," she said.

"So long," I repeated without interest.

"Shame we never got to know each other better," she purred.

"Shame you're a *deranged she-bitch!*" injected Flynn — somewhat uncharitably, I thought, if not entirely untruthfully.

Tara smiled. She bent toward me and kissed my cheek. (And, in the interest of complete and embarrassing disclosure, nibbled my ear a little.) *"Au revoir, mon cher,"* she breathed into my ear.

She leaned back on her heels and turned to Bruce. "Make it long and painful, Luther. Whatever *it* is..." She smiled like something swirling out of the mists of the Ark of the Covenant. "...Make it *long* and *painful*."

She and Time fell into the forced laughter of villains who can't come up with better exit lines. Time wrapped her arm in his. "We're off!" he said gaily, then patted his coat pocket. "Never fear, Luther! Ten minutes or so — *kablooey!*"

He pulled Tara lightly after him. "Come, m'dear!"

They ran off into the darkness like two lovers on the beach.

*   *   *

The journey back to Luther's headquarters cave reminded me
— if one can be reminded of that which one has never experienced — of what it must have been like for a B-17's tailgunner
over Berlin. Being cramped into the front seat between Luther
on my right and two black robes on my left, one of whom did
the driving, was bad enough, but the fumes and the relentlessly earsplitting echo of the diesel engine combined to make
the experience the kind of thing you wake up in a cold sweat
remembering twenty years later.

The headlights didn't glow so much as meekly glimmer
— we couldn't see what was ten feet in front of us until it was
two feet behind us. On several occasions the driver sputtered
(it requires a healthy breath to scream, and in that heady, confined atmosphere there could be no such thing as a healthy
breath) "Oh, no!" and spun the steering wheel wildly, causing
our dimly-lit view out the windshield to shift crazily to the
right or to the left. Then the driver would clutch at the wheel
for dear life as the passageway straightened and the rest of us
jolted back to an upright position.

Between the careening of the cab and the never-ending
struggle that inhalation had become, I did snatch the occa-
sional glimpse of Bruce's face, and what I saw was a study in
cognition: his eyes had caught fast on a far-distant point toward which the truck, despite its many frenzied changes of
direction, appeared always to be heading, for Bruce's gaze
never faltered.

He remained set in this pose until we wrenched to a
rackety stop some ten minutes later in a large hollow that had
been turned into a makeshift garage. The driver pushed the
two-foot long brake pedal once, twice, thrice, and then a
fourth time before the brakes decided to finally do something
with their misspent lives, an ambition they instantly achieved,

bringing us from forty miles an hour to a slight backwards crawl in a little under three seconds. The other two trucks lumbered in beside us, their engines slowly churning down to an ominous drone, as we disembarked, haggard and wobbly and blurry-eyed.

Bruce sighed enthusiasticlessly. "Miles, come with me. You, you, you, take the other three up on the lawn. Use a pistol."

My heart jolted as if someone had cried "Clear!" and applied the paddles. The truth of the matter — that we, Peter, Gerald, Flynn, me, all of us, were about to solve the Great Mystery of Life, i.e., die — hit me solidly in the chest.

I looked at Flynn, who was looking back at me, his eyes saying, "Well, so long, old chap. I forgive you for getting me into this mess. See you soon in a better world!"

My eyes said back, "We're not dead yet, Flynn. Don't give up hope!"

His eyes replied indulgently, "The time comes when a man has to face facts, Miles, m'boy. We're going to die. Not the future I'd choose, I'll grant you, but, still, perhaps it's for the best."

"For the best?" said my eyes unbelievingly. "How can *death* be for the best?"

His eyes twinkled. "Miles, let's not let this, our final conversation, devolve into an argument. Let's go out as we came in — the best of friends!"

My eyes began to tear, and so did his, and that was our goodbye—

I turned on Bruce. "Don't do this," I said. "You're not a killer, you've never hurt anyone in your life — you can handle death in the abstract, but when it gets right down to it, when it comes to really, actually pulling the trigger, you're no more a murderer than I am!"

Bruce looked at me wearily. The life had gone out of him like a party going on five a.m. But he did contrive a small smile. "That's not technically true, Miles. I poisoned the guy who led the Western Wing before I did, and I helped *him* poison the guy who led the Western Wing before he did."

"Oh," I said, there being nothing much else for me to say.

"Look," he said, sharply showing some of his old spirit, "I'll make you a proposal. Join THE UNKNOWN — become co-leader with me of the Western Wing — and I'll spare your life." He pointed at the others. "I'll spare their lives, too — provided they join as well."

"When hell freezes ov — ow!" cried Flynn, after being spiked in the shin by Gerald.

Bruce began to pace. "This whole thing has turned into such a fiasco," he lamented. "I spend the better part of a year developing this grand design and Justin Time comes along and has it figured out in the better part of five minutes. Fact is, Miles, we could use your brain. Jeez, we could use *a* brain, period. We're just a bunch of hapless jokes in the Western Wing — no, it's true," he said as certain of the black robes moved forward, ready to dispute this self-slander. "Fury was right. We're bungling, ineffectual boobs! Especially compared to the Eastern Wing. They're all Jonas Salks and we're all Nutty Professors. We need new blood! We need a transfusion!"

He looked at me deferentially, imploringly. "You've got a great mind for this work, Miles Hudson. *You* could be somebody in THE UNKNOWN. *You* could be the man to take us into the twenty-first century. *You* could be the next great leader in world history. Alexander, Caesar, Napoleon, Frederick...*Miles Jeffrey Hudson.*"

He paused, glancing around the garage. After his speech I felt more in the mood to go out and crush the Notre Dame varsity squad than conquer the globe, but my situation was not one that called for quibbling — when the options are a) death and b) something short of death, I'll take option b) every time.

"What do you say?" he asked in a whisper, the way I imagine the same words were spoken by Lucifer to the assembled throng of discontented angels.

"Join or die," I said. "Join or die. —I could pretend to join, Bruce, just to save my skin. We could *all* pretend to join, just to save our skins."

"Was I not right about the great mind?" asked Bruce delightedly of this assembled throng. "Yes, you could pretend, Miles, and as plain stupid as we've proven to be, you'd more than likely get away with it, for a while. But why would you want to lie? I'm offering you the resources of the Western Wing of THE UNKNOWN! We may have mishandled them, but those resources *are* vast — unbeatable, in the right hands. The Western Wing is a mighty juggernaut that only wants a firm hand at the wheel. Take the wheel, Miles. *Take the wheel.*"

I would of course love to be able to report that I pluckily refused his offer and embraced my fate with a firm resolve — a fate which obviously I escaped some other way, or else this story wouldn't be told in the first person — but I cannot report that, because it did not happen.

What *did* happen was a burst of noise and heat from the canvassed-over beds of the three trucks, after which the world went black. My last coherent thought was, I'll bet those splinters of wood shooting toward me bear the remains of black stencils that once read *California Hobby Supplies, Ltd.*

CHAPTER XXXII
. . .SURPRISE

THE EXPRESSION "PARALYZED WITH PAIN" IS ONE THAT'S THROWN around rather loosely, to my mind, one of those pithy phrases a writer uses without the least idea as to what it's really like to be *paralyzed with pain*. The phrase itself is misleading, because it's not that you can't move for the pain, but that you *can* — just not without releasing an excruciating yowl.

Such was the condition in which I found myself. Conscious awareness returned slowly, during which time I foolishly attempted to stir various segments of my body. Each of these attempts resulted in a kind of anguish that would have made the Marquis de Sade uncomfortable, and also resulted in tiny grumbles of agony escaping my lips, grumbles the generation of which also brought fresh aches to my lungs, my vocal chords, my tongue, my lips. The human body suffers, I can reliably inform you, from no shortage of nerves.

I also felt wet. Saturated, in fact. My pants were plastered to my bare legs and the t-shirt under my button-down was heavy with dampness. My time underground had been humid, to be sure, but this was the equivalent of a full-body marinade. The first theory to spring to mind was *Blood!*, but this liquid lacked the viscosity of blood, and its sickening smell — though it did have that intense, pungent, special aroma that only standing water can acquire.

Lasting Lake.

I was drenched from head to toe in the waters of Lasting Lake.

Being exceedingly careful not to budge a single muscle, I explored the surface upon which I lay. Hard. Rough. Wet. Hard, rough, and wet, like the deck of...

I opened my eyes in an instant.

Queeg recoiled as if I was a cadaver and he was the coroner. "Yiiii!" he said. Then, recovering, "Great ghosts, Hudson, what's yer problem? Scare a man to death, why don't ya!"

The pain from my eyelids and eyeballs (yes, eyelids and eyeballs can and do feel pain) was fierce, but I managed to keep them barely slitted open. I took in the scene as my gaze would allow, inasmuch as my neck muscles refused to rotate with any speed, and what I saw was Queeg sprawled backwards to my right — he'd been bending over me until I frightened him by opening my eyes, at which point he'd tumbled rearward — and his three sons standing shyly to my left, keeping their distance, wringing their hands uncomfortably, failing in every way to maintain eye contact.

I was stretched out on my back on the main deck of the *Zuider Zee*. The boat's tall mast fingered into the blue above me, bobbing gently with the waves. The only sounds were those of Queeg's ponderous breathing and the cawing of a flock of birds high overhead. It was a peaceful, tranquil scene...one that I had far too little opportunity to enjoy before Queeg leaned back over me and said, "Hey now! We got to get you t' the medics, lad! Y'don't look good at all!"

I coughed, and sputtered, and emptied my lungs of a gallon or two of excess water. The pain by now was a kind of sunlight, everywhere, all-pervasive, but easy to take for granted and easy to shove into the background — but only because other questions were thankfully beginning to skywrite themselves across my consciousness, occluding the bright white ball of pain.

Just what the heck had happened?

Where were Flynn, Peter, Gerald?

Were they even alive?

What about Bruce? Had he survived?

How had I survived?

To the first of these questions I had a sneaking suspicion I already knew the answer. Justin Time had double-crossed Bruce, having at some point secreted the bombs in the trucks and later detonating them as he'd promised.

Why would he do this? I couldn't begin to hazard a guess, except that my mind slid right past the beginning and hazarded a guess: could Time have been one of those Eastern Wingers who wanted the feud between the wings to continue, or to end once and for all with the elimination of the Western Wing? It made as much sense as anything else during the last few days had.

To the last of the above questions I also believed I knew the answer. The explosion must either have blown a hole through the cavern walls, or weakened those walls to such an extent that they could no longer hold back the waters of Lasting Lake. In either case, those waters had flooded the cavern, sweeping me — and presumably Flynn, Peter, Gerald, Bruce, everyone in the cavern — away, through the underground river system, and up to the surface.

That I should have survived all this was testament, I theorized, to the essential impartiality of the universe. After everything it had thrown at me in such a relatively brief span, it felt I needed a break.

And it gave me, I would later discover, four of them: the *pisiform* and the second *carpal* of the right hand, the *cuboid* of the left foot, and the left third *costal*, or rib.

I heard Queeg grunt. His rugged, unshaven face came into view above me. "We been waitin' for two days, Hudson. We were 'bout ready to leave, and damn the consequences, when we saw ye floatin' by clutchin' a keyboard for buoyancy. Ye're damned lucky we hadn't already gone, man!"

I tried to sit up, the pain washing over me. Queeg wrapped his arms under my back and helped me lean upright.

There I glimpsed, over the railing, where Everlasting House had once stood, nothing but a smoking pile of ash.

"Oh, yeah," said Queeg, following my gaze, "we were also wonderin' if ye knew anything about *that*."

*   *   *

A well-known phenomenon, that of a sudden burst of adrenaline that enables you to lift the burning vehicle off of your wife, or disarm a villain twice your size, or leap from a boat and swim the twenty yards to shore despite injuries that would have sidelined Godzilla. That's what I did, and I take no credit for it, for it was all my body's doing, and I would no more say, "Look at me, I leapt from the boat and swam the twenty yards to shore!" than I would, "Look at me, my ears are hearing!" The reason was simply that the sight of a smoldering black hole where once had lived Everlasting House had triggered a physiological reaction which led to me dive over the side and freestyle my way to shore in under fifty seconds.

Which Queeg took in stride, opening his mouth to protest, but never getting the chance to speak, for I was already some distance from the *Zuider Zee*, kicking furiously through the depths. I heard him say, "Aye, ain't it the way. Save a man's life and there's the thanks ye get. Ah, well, let's weigh anchor and clear out, then."

I reached the shore and staggered up the beach, my mind refusing to believe what my eyes were stubbornly insisting was the truth: Everlasting House was now a pile of soot. An immense, Himalayan pile of soot, but a pile of soot nonetheless. Wisps of smoke snaked upwards from charred and crumbling embers that blanketed an area at least two acres square. The devastation was complete — not a wall nor a rafter was left standing. Everywhere the ground was black.

I fell to my knees, cursing the fate that had spared me but — it now appeared certain — claimed the lives of my friends. Viewing this devastating scene of destruction, my survival seemed all the more miraculous, and the survival of Peter, Gerald, or Flynn seemed resolutely impossible.

The explosion of the boat-bombs must only have weakened the underground walls, then, and they hadn't given way until the blazing fire started by the bombs had consumed Everlasting House. I could only marvel that the blazing fire hadn't consumed *me*, and therein lay some small measure of hope that if I survived, others might have, as well.

But looking at a giant black circle burned into the skin of the earth will tend to drive a man toward pessimism, and looking at that giant black circle, all I could think was, *They're gone.*

I stood, with difficulty, and stepped forward, shuffling my waterlogged penny loafers through the ashes of Everlasting House, which soon came up to mid-calf. My exertions were catching up to me. The superhumanizing effect of the adrenaline was wearing off, leaving me once more an awfully, awfully tired mortal. I didn't dare sit, or fall, in this soot, for fear of being swallowed up in it like quicksand, so I turned around and began a drudging path back to the lakeshore.

I hadn't gone far before a flash of light struck my eye. Not twenty feet away, off to the left — I turned and stamped toward it. It flashed again, glinting in the sun. It was small, about the size of a credit card, and gleamed silver — could it be? Is that what it was? —Could it be Officer Gerald's *badge?*

I hurried my pace, but with my next step the ground cracked and gave way beneath me. I dropped into murky darkness.

*   *   *

I remember everything about that fall. I could see nothing, and I was almost happy that my legs no longer had to support my weight, but I did realize that sooner or later every fall has an ending, and when it's human flesh doing the falling, that ending is more often than not an unpleasant one. Still, after the initial panicky thoughts of, *Boy, isn't this just typical of my day*, my mind reached a sort of repose, a placid fatalism that was unexpectedly comforting. I would leave this earth behind, but I would do it quickly and relatively painlessly, and since my body would likely never be found, it would be assumed that I had died along with the others in the cataclysm that had devoured Everlasting House. Not the greatest of deaths, but not the worst, either; and I could, by stretching the truth only a little, rightfully claim that while THE UNKNOWN got me in the end, I did take a bunch of 'em with me.

Thus I plummeted to my certain death in a pensive, contemplative mood.

*   *   *

But nothing in life — or death — is certain. Except perhaps that a hundred-foot plunge *hurts*, even when it's broken by a trampoline-like trapeze net spread across the floor of the cavern.

The breath was knocked from me, and my chest erupted in agony. My limbs were soothed to a gentle stop, then ricocheted back up into the air, even as I asked myself, "Who would spread a trampoline-like trapeze net across the floor a hundred feet beneath the surface?"

I bounced up and down a few times before coming to a shuddering halt. My body, which I wouldn't have believed could take any more, had taken seconds, thirds, and an extra helping of dessert. I lay there, immobile, and in no way anxious ever to regain mobility, my arms and legs outstretched on the bungee-like material that made up the net. I took a deep breath, but because of the broken rib, I immediately wished it had been a shallow breath.

Can't I do anything without it hurting? I asked myself.

Try wiggling your toe.

...No, that hurts too. Why do I even bother to listen to you anymore?

At that moment two strong arms reached from out of the darkness around me like a zombie's from the grave. I squealed as they grabbed hold of my shoulders, but all that came from my exhausted lungs was a dull whine. The arms pulled me up and out, the pain causing a delirium that blacked me out momentarily.

When I came to I had been placed in a curiously familiar easy chair. My chest was still protesting every subtle motion of even the remotest part of my body, but against this I clenched my teeth and succeeded in opening my eyes and swiveling my head about. Tall bookshelves rose around me like pillars...bookshelves filled with row after row of dusty, ancient tomes of all sizes and colors...and before me, a globe, about three feet in diameter...and on the end table to my right, Patrick Hester's leather-bound diary.

I was in the library.

"Welcome back," said an amiable voice, a voice which I almost didn't recognize, thanks to the strength and resolve it had lately taken to exhibiting.

I almost grinned, though that would have been wildly inappropriate.

"Hey, Dr. Humphreys."

*   *   *

"We haven't much time," he said calmly, removing his spectacles to clean them with his handkerchief as he'd done before. "I'll try to be succinct." He replaced the glasses on his thin nose and leaned forward in his chair, propping his forearms on his thighs. "I'm afraid you never did have a true appreciation of what you were up against, Miles. Who we are — what we are — what we've been — what we've done — what we're capable of. The fact that you never did gain that true appreciation is due exclusively, I think I can say without false immodesty, to *my* machinations."

He smiled like a grandfather. (Which, come to think of it, he was.) "You can't profess an overabundance of common sense, my boy, but you can rightfully brag to a keen enough mind — so I'll provide a few answers and leave it to you to divine the rest."

I nodded vaguely, unsure whether he was expecting a response. To be honest, I was surprised anybody would still be of the opinion I had a "keen enough" mind, given how far behind the curve of events I'd apparently been, all along the way.

He said, "To begin with: Justin did set up Luther, as you must have already guessed. After you clapped Luther on the side of the head, Justin — with the assistance of three dozen friends — transferred the boats into the trucks. He assured me that he would detonate the bombs well clear of Everlasting House, but either he was lying to me or things went unspeakably wrong."

A steely spark glittered in his eyes. "For that, I will never *quite* be able to forgive Mr. Justin Time. Everlasting

House was my home for many years. I am enormously sorry to see it go."

He suddenly smiled. "Not that we're not well-rid of Luther, mind you. We've all grown weary of that motor-mouthed dunderhead — one 'grand design' after another, each more absurd than the last. When he came to us with this bomb idea my immediate reaction was, 'Spare me,' but after some consideration I realized this bomb idea was the perfect solution to the problem of What To Do About Luther."

He sighed. "If only Justin hadn't screwed it up. Or screwed me over. Whichever applies."

He slapped me on the knee. "But you lived, which is good."

Gee, thanks, I thought.

"I always was fond of you, Miles, even before all of this occurred, but in the past several days you've displayed a steadfast determination I never suspected you of possessing. It's made me admire you all the more.   Truthfully, we couldn't have asked for a more implacable foe."

I shrugged self-effacingly, as I wasn't sure how else to respond. Why was it that everyone connected to THE UNKNOWN found me such a likable guy? Imagine their feelings toward me if I'd been trying to destroy their conspiracy or something.

"A couple of other things just before you go," Dr. Humphreys continued. "In future don't ever assume that you're in control — that it's *your* hand guiding events. I told you before and I'll tell you again: you do not begin to grasp the reach of our influence and power. If you should ever find yourself wondering why this or that happened at just the right time, or just the wrong time, it's not serendipity, it's not providence — it's *us*. THE UNKNOWN."

He smiled that Grandpa Walton smile again. "To clear up two mysteries, before you ask: It was Luther who ordered the poisoning of Tara — much against the wishes of cooler heads, including myself. After your refusal to give the handshake or take the house, he flew into a fright — if you weren't the emissary, who was? He settled on Tara as the likeliest suspect, since she'd just arrived from Atlanta, longtime seat of the Eastern Wing. He further convinced himself that after so many months of failing to detect the emissary, the best way to impress the Eastern Wing was not to *expose* the emissary, but to *do away with* the emissary...yes, good old Luther's logic, impeccable as always.

"He had her poisoned, then, as you surmised — oh, I've been reading your notes, I should have mentioned that — and as you also surmised, you were poisoned in the hospital in the hopes that you would never have the opportunity to warn Tara of the danger she was facing. Luther wanted you dead in any case, of course, which is why he sent the snipers and the midnight assassin after you, but if Tara *was* the emissary and you *did* warn her, then Luther feared she would call in the vast resources of the Eastern Wing to protect her, and Luther would have been humiliated and likely ousted by his own people. Including, again" — he smiled impishly — "me."

"How," I asked, "is someone that incompetent allowed to remain in charge of half a global conspiracy?"

Dr. Humphreys laughed. "First of all, the only thing the Western Wing is half of is maybe one per cent of our global ventures, and that's being generous."

The Western Wing accounts for only half of one per cent, I thought, *of the global ventures of* THE UNKNOWN? *That means if I want to stop the whole conspiracy I'll have to go through this 200 more times!*

"Luther wasn't exaggerating," Dr. Humphreys went on, "when he told you the Western Wing suffers from an inferiority complex — it's well-deserved. They've been led by a series of buffoons from the beginning. Luther's just the latest, and, to tell you the truth, he's no worse than any of the others. But no better, either."

"Aren't you," I asked, "a member of the Western Wing? You talk about them like you're an outsider."

He leaned back in his chair. "I hold something of a...unique...position, Miles. I am a part of THE UNKNOWN, but I also remain outside of it, insofar as I can. I live — well, *lived* — in my house and I perform — *performed* — my studies in secret, here in my library, intruding on UNKNOWN business only when I deemed it absolutely necessary."

"This is *your* library?"

He smiled, but didn't answer the question. "I did have to move a few things around," he said, "to make room for the net. I'm sure the question has occurred to you...why was there a net placed in precisely the proper spot to break your fall? Because, Miles, you were bound to come exploring the cinders of Everlasting House — you're like a cat, your curiosity always does get the better of you — and it was a straightforward matter to position a platform of rotted plywood under a layer of soot, then place Gerald's badge above it to draw you in."

He spread his hands. "Spread a web, catch a fly."

A cough erupted from his throat. He covered his mouth. "I'm getting older. The dust and the temperature down here afflict me more than they used to. May not be such a bad thing that the house is gone, after all."

He stood. "I'll have to say my goodbyes—"

"No!" I cried hoarsely, sitting forward in my chair. "What about—"

"Your friends? Are they alive or dead?" He put his hand on my shoulder. "I know you have questions, Miles. Many of them. Your birth certificate, for instance. Is it real or is it fake? And if it's real, what does it mean, that it was here in this library?"

From out of nowhere, a syringe appeared in his other hand, and shot forward to plunge into my bicep. I let out a cry of protest, but it was too late. The syringe had already been emptied into my veins.

"Relax, it's only a sedative." He tossed the syringe into a nearby trash bin. "I'm not going to answer any of your questions, Miles. Because I want you to answer them for yourself. I've read your notes — you're a good historian, a good detective. You'll make an excellent chronicler. You'll follow the clues and in time, you'll figure everything out."

A fuzzy haze was falling across my line of sight. I fought to stay awake. "Why are you letting me live?" I croaked. "I'll tell what I know! I'll expose THE UNKNOWN!"

"I'm counting on that," he said with a smile. "No one will believe you at first, but you'll keep plugging away. It's in your nature."

Through blurry eyes I looked at Dr. Humphreys for the first time for who he really was: a dominating manipulator of events. Try as I might, though, I was still unable to work up a good frothing dislike of the man...just as THE UNKNOWN had found me annoyingly likable, I had found them — Bruce, Justin, Dr. Humphreys — a frustratingly likable bunch, as well.

"I was wrong about you," I said, the sedative making my voice husky. "You had me convinced you were a nobody in the organization, nothing but a flunky."

He pursed his lips demurely. "All part of the act."

"But in actuality you're the ringleader."

He raised an eyebrow. "Oh, no, not the ringleader. But 126 years do bring with them a certain authority."

This took a moment to sink in. Although "burst in like a locomotive" is a more appropriate analogy than "sink in."

"126 years?" I asked, eyes wide, heart pounding. My glance went automatically to the diary at my side. One final revelation to set my mind reeling.

"You're...Patrick Hester...?"

He tilted his head in a gesture that may have been acknowledgement, or may have been denial.

"But..." I struggled for words. "But...that can't be..."

The sedative was too strong. I could fight it no longer.

"I started this," I heard him whisper as I quickly drifted into the most agreeable slumber of my lifetime, "and I'm going to end it. *With your help.*"

With these words, so full of portent, so full of objectionability, the shortest day of my life drew to a close.

CHAPTER XXXIII
A PLAN

FOR THE THIRD TIME IN THREE DAYS I AWOKE FROM AN UNCONSCIOUS state. For the second time in three days I did that awakening within the bleak gray walls of Perpetual Hospital. What was worse, Chief Detective Superintendent Chauncey was sitting beside my bed, a pipe between his lips and *Hondo* by Louis L'Amour between his fingers. It was enough to make a man long for an extended coma.

"Ah, you're awake, then," he said jovially, setting down the book and removing his pipe. "Doc said it'd happen any-time."

"Should you be smoking in here?" I asked irritably. My mood — which I cannot excuse but can easily explain by re-questing that you reread the past few chapters — was foul.

Chauncey looked at his pipe as if the possibility that it might prove offensive had never once crossed his mind in all his years. "It's not lit," he said. "But if you like, I'll put it away." He slipped it into his inside coat pocket. "Better?"

"Have you found Flynn? Peter? Gerald?"

Chauncey pressed forward, his face suddenly serious. "We found you underneath an elm tree not far from the ruins of Everlasting House, laid out with your arms folded across your chest. We found Gerald — who's in Room 409, right next door, he was bruised all over, couple of broken bones, waterlogged, injuries consistent with yours — out by Lasting Lake. We found no one else."

I gaped at him. "What do you mean, *'no one else'*?"

"The usual meaning," he answered. "I mean that we found *no one else*."

"No one else *alive*?"

"No one else, period."

"No *bodies*?"

"No one else *period*, Dr. Hudson."

"But — the bomb…the fire…"

"Our arson team has determined that the House was destroyed by a large cache of TNT set off in an underground cavern. The cavern subsequently flooded, but not before the fire spread to the above-ground structure. We've not found one trace of another human being, Dr. Hudson."

"But there were dozens, hundreds of them—"

"Yes, I know," said Chauncey, now leaning back. "Gerald's given me the entire story. Can't say it's an easy story to swallow, but when you've got evidence of a truckload of dynamite and a historic house goes down in flames, you kind of have to take whatever story you can get."

"But where did all the bodies *go*? My best friend was down there! And dozens of other people!"

"Can't answer you that," said Chauncey, absentmindedly removing his pipe and tapping his lip with its stem. "Gerald assures me there were at least 200 of these UNKNOWN conspirators underneath Everlasting House at the time of the explosion. The only reason I have to doubt his word — and yours, for that matter — is that it's no easy task to collect and dispose of 200 corpses when emergency crews are swarming over the location."

Something was pinging at the back of my brain, *something—*

"Wait!" I exclaimed. "The library!"

"It's fine," he said. "Downtown. Long, long ways from the blast."

"Not the City Library, the library at Everlasting House! It survived the fire, I was there *after* the fire!"

I told him of my plunge, and of my chat with Dr. Humphreys. When I got to the part about Humphreys' true identity, Chauncey's eyes took on a peculiar, stunned glint.

"Patrick *Hester?*" said the Chief Detective Superintendent.

"That's right," I replied. "He's kept himself alive all these years. Don't ask me how."

Chauncey scratched his ear. He was blinking rapidly. His eyes darted to and fro about the room, presumably because they were not receiving the slightest instruction from his brain, which was obviously overoccupied elsewhere. After a significant while, they settled on me.

"Did it occur to you that maybe he wasn't being completely honest?" he asked. "Or that he wasn't being completely *sane?*" He stood up quickly, bracing his temples with the thumb and forefinger of his left hand. "Alive for *126 years?* It's ludicrous!"

"So are 200 bodies disappearing and so is Everlasting House burning down and so is the whole concept of THE UNKNOWN," I said. "You're going to have to face the fact that 'ludicrous' does not mean 'impossible.' Lord knows *I've* had to. There *is* an UNKNOWN conspiracy, and we've stopped it here in Constant, but Constant's nothing but a hair on a wart on an elephant. They are — literally — everywhere. There's a tremendous lot of work left to do, Chauncey, and you, me, and Gerald are the only ones left to do it."

During the middle of this outburst Chauncey had begun to stare at me again with that same stunned expression.

"Even if you're right, why not quit while you're ahead? You've beat them here, you've driven them away from Constant — you've won! Why antagonize them further? Haven't they convinced you they're *serious*, already?"

I tried to look as indomitable, as dauntless, as a man can when he's lying flat on his back. "I'm serious, too," I said, my strained throat giving my voice the same inflections Clint Eastwood's enjoys naturally. "I don't know if Flynn and Peter are dead or alive, and that's reason enough for me to continue. And I know right where to begin — Topeka, Kansas."

"Topeka?" said Chauncey. "Why Topeka? There's nothing in Topeka. I've been there, I should know."

"My parents live there."

"Well, I meant nothing but them, of course. But how do your parents pertain?"

"The birth certificate, Chauncey." His eyes glowed with realization. "My parents must have some idea why Patrick Hester had it stashed away in his underground library."

"You don't think your parents are in on it, do you?"

"I don't know," I said. "One thing I have most assuredly learned — trust no one."

"Not even your own parents?"

"Unfortunately no."

"Then there's no hope of talking you out of pursuing this?"

"There's no hope, Chauncey."

He sat back down, the chair's legs creaking. "What a mess. —Well, I'll help in any way I can, but that won't be much. I can't leave Constant. I'm the Chief Detective Superintendent."

"If I need anything I'll be sure to let you know. One favor you can do for me."

"What's that?"

"Persuade Gerald to come with me."

"No problem there, Dr. Hudson," said Officer Gerald, standing in the doorway in his hospital gown, five or six dozen tubes trailing after him down the hall. "They tried to blow me up, and I am a *police officer*. I *want* these guys."

He smiled grimly, reached out his hand, and took a step toward me. Then he tripped on one of his tubes and crashed to the floor.

*   *   *

Two days later I returned to clear out my office at Constant College. The campus was all but vacant, sealed off as it had been by the authorities. Fully 80 per cent of the faculty — including Peter Cranston, Yuri Zelikov, Rachel Gutierrez, Walter Hendricks, and even the Dean, Dr. Franklin Allen Humphreys — had disappeared under the most mysterious of circumstances. Everlasting House, for decades the proudest landmark of the town of Constant, could now be swept up in a child's pail.

As long as that child was fifty feet tall.

It was all more than sufficient grist for even the rustiest of gossip-mills. People's greetings had turned from "Hello!" to "Have you heard?" The town was at a standstill; the populace was in shock.

On orders from Chauncey I was forbidden to tell what I knew. I wasn't all that anxious to share what I knew in any event, because the moment I did I'd have been branded either delusional (Justin Time's prediction come true) or a celebrity — and the second possibility frightened me more than the first. I was under no illusion that I was not now Enemy Number One of THE UNKNOWN, and that they would seek their revenge in their own good time. But knowing yourself that you are a marked man and hearing an anchorperson declare that you a marked man are two very different things.

So I wound my way across the campus, trying to avoid the clusters of students and staff that were present (small groups were being given limited access to the campus), keeping what conversations I did have short and impersonal. Yes, it certainly was a bizarre situation. No, I had no idea what could have happened to Dr. Fill-In-The-Name. Yes, I was sure the police had everything well in hand.* Yes, things should settle down in a couple of days. Yes, it would be very interesting to see how the Board of Regents handled things — especially with four of its members among the missing.

My office remained as I had left it, an eternity ago. The big clock on the wall read 10:14. Had this been a normal college day, I would have been deeply immersed in my American Colonial History class, debating the merits and demerits of mercantilism. The students would be pretending to care, and I would be pretending I hadn't moderated the same debate dozens of times before.

I set the two boxes I'd brought with me on the floor, then my briefcase on the desk, and cast my eyes over the office. Like Dr. Humphreys', it was drowning in books. I had more than I needed — more than I could read in a lifetime. Textbooks, source material, magazines, encyclopedias, almanacs, even a stack of novels.

This is your life, I thought. *Or, this was your life. 27 years, and this to show for it. Your life hasn't been a life so much as it's been a lesson plan.*

From the office's sole window, which I hadn't remembered leaving open, came the sound of a couple of students chattering excitedly amongst themselves as they crossed the lawn outside. The trees in the courtyard swayed in the breeze,

---

* It will be noted that I had long ago moved beyond being a liar of uncommon caliber — my rank was now that of "Cuban Ambassador."

rustling a soft song. The sun shone down warmly on the living and the presumed-dead.

I'll find you, Flynn, I said, but not out loud. *I know you're still alive. I don't know how I know, but I know. I'll find you, Flynn. I'll find you, Peter. However long it takes.*

And I'll find you, too, Dr. Humphreys! Or Patrick Hester, or whoever you are. And you, too, Tara Fury, and you, too, Justin Time!

I'll find you all. I have a plan.

Yeah, right! said the little voice inside my head, which I would gladly have murdered if in doing so I would not also have murdered myself. *You had a plan before, remember? Look how brilliantly that turned out.*

This is different, I said back. *I've learned my lesson.*

Is that so? sneered the voice. *So this new one might be called a "lesson plan"?*

The voice chortled, amused by its own joke.

No, I countered. *Not a lesson plan. A regular old-fashioned not-a-chance-in-hell-it'll-work type of plan.* I smiled. *The best kind.*

It was as I was speaking these very words in my mind that I caught sight of the wall behind me, over my shoulder. I couldn't say why, exactly, this happened — an inexplicable impulse directed me, pulling my gaze to the right, beyond the door, back toward the wall behind my desk. The big clock was there, high up on the wall, and I asked myself, *Why did I put the clock behind me? I have to turn around every time I want to see what time it is.*

But I was only asking myself this to avoid having to ask myself a different question, and that question was:

How did my Professor Of The Month Award get up there on the wall?

Because there it was, shining and spotless, impeccably situated and perfectly level, impossible to miss except for a person whose mind was so preoccupied he wouldn't have noticed a slap on the face.

For that's what it was — that's what it had to be. A slap on the face. A shot across my bow. An unmistakable message from THE UNKNOWN: *We see you. We are everywhere. You cannot escape.*

Humphreys/Hester had not been exaggerating. My old life was over. My new life had begun.

I glanced at my briefcase, which held my notebook — my ongoing record of that new life. A chronicler, Humphreys/Hester had called me.

He wants me to write my story. But why?

I reached up and plucked down the plaque. *It's not a bad-looking award,* I thought. *That might be real silver, or at least real silver plating. I'd have been proud to receive this, if it were given for legitimate reasons. Wouldn't I?*

The old you would have been, I answered myself. *But you're not Dr. Miles Hudson, Professor of History, any more. You're Miles Hudson, regular guy, on an irregular mission. You've got friends to save, and enemies to vanquish.*

The voice started to make a snide and derisive comment, but I'd had enough of the voice for one day. I shushed it with a hiss.

Careful, I said, *or I'll leave you out of the book.*

I toed the top off of one of the boxes I'd brought and tossed the Professor of the Award inside. It landed with a thud. I thought of Peter's sixteen awards, languishing in his attic. Or was it seventeen?

"I'll find you," I said out loud, though I was talking to myself. "I have a plan."

Here ends the first packet of
the papers of Miles Hudson, Ph.D.

The second packet, Road to Nowhere,
chronicles his ongoing quest to unravel the mysteries
behind THE UNKNOWN, *his own identity,*
and what became of his friends.
Also, the transcendent menace of "the Thrombulator."

ABOUT THE AUTHOR

JAMES E. SARVER was born in Riverside, California, in 1969.

He has not been back since.

You are welcome to visit the author at:

www.jamesesarver.com

But please be very quiet, as he is usually sleeping.